THE MAKING OF
JOSHUA COBB

BY MARGARET HODGES

One Little Drum
What's for Lunch, Charley?
A Club against Keats
Tell It Again:
Great Tales from Around the World *(editor)*
The Secret in the Woods
The Wave
The Hatching of Joshua Cobb
Constellation *(editor)*
Sing Out, Charley!
Lady Queen Anne
The Making of Joshua Cobb

THE MAKING OF
JOSHUA COBB

MARGARET HODGES

ILLUSTRATED BY W. T. MARS

FARRAR, STRAUS AND GIROUX · NEW YORK
AN ARIEL BOOK

J
H

FOR FLETCHER AND THE BOYS

1

Now he knew who he was, and where he was, and why. He was Joshua Cobb. This was Oakley School, and he was running a mile around the Yard as the penalty for being late to breakfast.

A week ago, just after his twelfth birthday, he had traveled three hundred miles from home by bus to the little town of Oakley. With a dozen other boys from a dozen other places he had walked the road from the town to the school, carrying his suitcase and guitar. The road crossed a bridge over the Mohican River,

1

passed through the school grounds, and disappeared around a curve in the hills beyond the school farm.

Josh was still not used to being away at school. This morning when the rising bell had rung in the hall outside his room, he had not known who he was or where he was. In the gray light of early morning his roommate, Larry Dunlap, was a silent lump under the blankets of the other bed, invisible except for a mop of longish, straight blond hair and a sharp nose. Josh had closed his eyes again and determined to keep them closed until he heard Larry getting up.

That was one thing he had decided in this first week at Oakley School. Never get up when the first bell rings. Play it cool, like Larry. Wait for the second bell, the one that rang urgently, five minutes before breakfast. Then leap out of bed, jump into pants, shirt, jacket, socks, and shoes. Tie your tie on your way, at top speed, to the dining hall. If everything went exactly right, you could be standing in your place at your table before the headmaster started to say grace. One second late, and the dining-hall door was shut in your face. In that event, you found yourself jogging four times around the Yard before you could eat.

He jogged past North Hall, where he and Larry roomed on the first floor with the rest of the Fifth Form, the youngest class. Why hadn't he got up when he heard the others running by in the corridor? They were too scared, or too smart, to take a chance on being late. Josh had taken that chance because he followed Larry's lead as much as he could. At the last possible moment he had leaped out of bed and said, "Hey, we're late. Time to start hurrying." Larry had opened his eyes, grunted, and said, "Not yet." Then he had closed his eyes again.

Now Josh was on his second lap around the Yard, passing a couple of other late risers who were not as fast runners as he was, or maybe not as hungry. He jogged past South Hall, where he would be spending the morning in classes after breakfast, if he finally got in to breakfast. He hoped he was ready for Mr. Bishop's history class. Josh liked T.B., short for Thomas Bishop, because his class was really interesting. They were talking about ancient Rome, and whether those days were like these days. In those days, T.B. said, you were either an aristocrat, important and rich, or you were a plebeian, one of the common people. Unless, of course, you were a slave. There were no slaves at Oakley, but there certainly were aristos and plebes, and it was not hard, Josh thought, to figure out who were the aristos and who were the plebes. He had talked about it to a couple of other Fifth Formers and they had agreed.

Larry Dunlap was an aristo, and so was Mead Balfour. Denny Cheswick and Van Stevens were also definitely on Josh's list of aristos in the Fifth Form. When the time came to elect class officers, they would be in for sure.

Josh was a plebe. There were more plebes than aristos in ancient Rome, but Josh thought that prac-

3

tically everyone at Oakley was an aristo, except himself and a very few others. He saw Howie Howland coming out of the dining hall now, on his way to some early job and looking full of breakfast as Josh ran past. Howie was a plebe, and so were Scotty Scott and Jerry Loomis, all in the Fifth Form.

There were a lot of guys he didn't know yet, plus a lot who were so different that he could not put them in any group. There were several black boys, like Gordon Graham, who came from Harlem. And there were a couple of boys from somewhere in Asia. One boy, Ali Mahmud, came from the Middle East and was already known as Ali Baba. According to rumor, he could speak four languages, but nobody really believed this.

It did not take long to earn a nickname at Oakley. The faculty had theirs—T.B. Bishop, for example. Mr. Lowe, who taught English and coached the glee club, took special care of the Fifth Form. ("Wash your face, brush your teeth, comb your hair.") He was known as "Swing" Lowe. Mr. St. Clair, the headmaster, was "The Saint."

Josh was fully expecting to be called Corn Cobb. It had happened before, when he went to school at home, and once in a while at Camp Buddy, where he had gone for two summers. He didn't mind. But it was funny how much he did mind discovering that he was a plebe. He had never thought of such a thing before. At home, people were just people.

He was starting his last round of the Yard. There

4

would still be time to eat breakfast when he got to the dining hall, but he certainly would not be late again because of waiting for Larry Dunlap to get up. He would play it cool, but not that cool. As for dressing, he was probably the fastest dresser on campus, because he was stuck with exactly one suit—the one he was wearing when he arrived from home. None of his other clothes looked right.

It was a terrible way to start school, especially when your roommate had a whole closet full of great clothes. Josh had never thought much about clothes before, but now he thought about them a lot. One way to recognize an aristo was by his clothes. It was not the only way, but it helped. Josh's clothes did not look like Larry's. He shouldn't care, but he couldn't help it. He had never felt anything like this before. And besides all his other clothes, Larry had already bought a school blazer, dark green with gold buttons. Josh had come to school with one new suit and some old ones. Something told him that he could not ask for another new jacket so soon, but he wished he had one. Wearing Oakley blazers, no one looked better than anyone else.

He finished his mile several seconds ahead of the other late risers and sprinted into the building that housed the dining hall, where two hundred boys were munching cereal, hot breads, and bacon, under a dull roar of conversation and a clatter of crockery. He found his place at one of the long tables. "Gilly," Mr. McGill, who taught mathematics, frequently sat at the head of Josh's table. This morning, checking a list of names as Josh sat down, he said, "Done your mile? Fast time, Cobb. Someone pass him the cereal."

Josh filled his bowl and poured in milk to the brim.

Consulting his list again, Mr. McGill asked, "Where's Dunlap?"

Josh gulped down a mouthful and answered cautiously, "I don't know, sir."

"Not in the infirmary?"

"No, sir."

Mr. McGill raised his eyebrows and said, "Pass the cornbread to Cobb."

Corn . . . Cobb. Across the table a boy laughed, his dark eyes squinting behind black horn-rimmed glasses. Everybody else at the table looked at Josh. Sooner or later the old nickname always turned up. But the boy who had laughed had a funny name too. He was Igor Brilovich, and he had instantly been labeled Brillo, the Mad Russian. He could draw and paint like anything. Josh regarded Brillo with awe and liked him. When Brillo laughed, Josh grinned back at him.

Mr. McGill glanced at his wristwatch and announced, "Seven-thirty. A reminder to Fifth Formers: you have half an hour to make your beds, put your rooms in order, and do your jobs. I'll see you at assembly."

A bell rang. At the end of the room, at the head table, chairs were being pushed back, and Josh saw the headmaster standing with a group of other masters and three prefects, the top boys at Oakley School.

"Dismissed," said Mr. St. Clair.

When Josh reached North Hall he met Larry on the way out of their room with a candy bar in one hand and a toothbrush in the other. He looked at Josh coldly and said, "Why didn't you wake me up?"

"I did," Josh told him. "It wasn't my fault if you went back to sleep." He edged past and began making his bed. He wondered what it would be like to have a candy bar for breakfast.

"Some roommate," Larry said resentfully. Then he shrugged and added, "It doesn't matter. I hate breakfast." He headed off down the corridor toward the washroom.

Josh straightened his side of the room by clearing his desk and dresser. Then he got a big push broom from the storage closet across the hall and swept the corridor. He had just finished when Larry passed him, carrying a small broom to clean the stairs that led down from the upper floor. He did not speak or look at Josh.

Josh put away his broom and started for the auditorium, walking fast and feeling bad all over. Would Larry still be mad when they had to sit next to each other at Job Assembly? Rooming with a guy who didn't even like him—how could he stand that for a whole year? His fears were confirmed when Larry sat down beside him in the auditorium five minutes later without saying a word.

During assembly, the Fifth Form sat in the front rows of the auditorium, with the older Forms behind them and the First Form officers and prefects on the platform facing all of them. The Head Prefect, Alan Crane, made announcements while First Form inspectors were making the rounds of the school. Every boy at Oakley had a daily job assigned to him. It might be cleaning washrooms, corridors, or stairs. It might be cutting grass or raking leaves. The dining-hall tables had to be set up and then cleared three times a day, after which someone had to run the big dishwasher. With two hundred boys to share the work, it was easy, if everyone did his job right. There were penalties for jobs done sloppily, or left undone. Today, Crane announced, anyone on detention would go by truck to the school farm to dig potatoes.

Except for the trouble with Larry, Josh's mind was at ease. He had swept his corridor well and there was no reason to think that he would be on detention. He could look forward to the first football practice, which would take place in the Lower Field after classes, according to Alan Crane's announcement.

The job inspectors came back and handed up slips of paper. "Gilly" contributed one of his own.

Crane began, "This is the end of the first week of school. We are off to a pretty good start. I just want to remind all of you, especially the Fifth Form, that the school rules are posted on the bulletin board. You are supposed to learn them. Some rules are more important than others, but your business is not to break any of them. One is that no one goes into town without permission. This is important. The school is responsible for every boy and someone in authority has to know where you are at all times. Mr. Marvell saw a boy crossing the bridge toward town yesterday. He does not know who it was, but no one had permission to go into town yesterday. Any questions?" There were no questions.

"Now, for those who are on detention today." An anxious hush settled over the auditorium. Fifth Form offenders were read off first, and Josh was not surprised to hear, "Dunlap, absent from breakfast." But he could not believe his ears when he heard, "Cobb, unsatisfactory job in the North Hall corridor, first floor."

What could be wrong? He knew he had not left dirt on that floor. As soon as Job Assembly ended, he headed back to his corridor to take a look. There was no doubt about it. On the floor under the stairs lay some bits of paper and woolly gray rolls of dust. He did not see how he could have missed them.

It was not until he was sweeping them into a dustpan that he figured it out. Larry had swept the dirt off the stairs and let it fall on Josh's clean floor. Josh wondered if Larry had done it on purpose. He wondered even more when Larry passed him in the corridor a minute later and said, "Ha!"

"You dropped this dirt," Josh said.

"Sorry about that. Who made me late for breakfast?"

With a full dustpan Josh followed him down the corridor. "Sorry about that," he called. "See you in the potato field." He couldn't help laughing to him-self.

Larry's answer was, "See you on the farm, Corn Cobb."

2

The potato field turned out to be the best fun that
Josh had had since he came to Oakley School. "Captain" Marvell, a popular master who had a skin-head
haircut, was in charge of the squad. In an old army
shirt and pants, he worked along with them for a
while, then drove off in the school truck, leaving them
to finish the job on their own. From that point on,
the potato squad spent as much time throwing potatoes as they spent digging them. Josh and Larry
singled each other out for targets. There were plenty

11

of misses but also a few good satisfying hits, which seemed to cancel out grievances. When Mr. Marvell returned, the squad was in fine fettle and worked with a will for two hours to fill the truck, ride back to the dining hall, and heave out the sacks at the kitchen door.

As they were leaving the truck, dust-covered, sore, and weary, but in high good humor, Brillo Brilovich walked past. He was wearing a new jacket and his shoes were shined. "Coolie labor," he said to Josh, looking at the lumpy sacks.

"Sure is," Josh said. They headed toward North Hall. "Where have you been? Didn't you go to football practice?"

"No," said Brillo. "Football's not my kind of thing. Three of us went to Swing Lowe and got permission to work on the farm squad instead. It's coolie labor too, really, but it's better than football. Swing invited us for tea."

"Tea?" said Josh. "Just tea?"

"And cookies," Brillo told him. "He played some good records for us too. First he tried to talk us into changing our minds. But we didn't give in, so he said we could pick apples and pitch hay and stuff like that."

"I want to play football," Josh said.

Football was one reason he was glad to be at Oakley School, glad that his mother had talked him into coming here instead of going to high school at home. He remembered how she had put it.

"I had a letter today from Mr. St. Clair at Oakley School. You know, your father went to Oakley, and if he were living I think he'd like you to go there too. There are some scholarships. It's a great opportunity, Josh. I think you ought to try out for one of those scholarships. It could be the making of you. It's a chance to get a fine education, and you'd know boys from all over the country and all over the world. Besides there are hills and a river at Oakley instead of city streets. I think you'd like that."

Josh had asked, "Could I play football?"

"Even more than in a big high school. I really think you'll like it."

But Josh did not like Oakley all the time. He had never known there could be so many rules and penalties. He seemed to be always breaking some rule or other and paying penalties. He could not even eat his dinner without worrying. As a Fifth Former he had to learn the school song and be ready to sing it at dinner on demand. He had to know and be able to tell at dinner how many days, hours, minutes, and seconds were left before the big varsity football game played against Newton at Thanksgiving. He worked out a beautiful time chart with all the necessary figures and then lost it the very night a First Former pounced on him with, "Cobb, how many days, hours, minutes, and seconds until the Newton game?" He had to polish the First Former's shoes for not knowing the answer. And a few of the First Formers were definitely mean. He minded his own business and kept away from them. They made him think uneasily about Red Bullock, a counselor who had made his life miserable during his first summer at Camp Buddy.

Also, he wished that Mr. McGill did not sit so often at the head of his table. Mr. McGill taught algebra to the Fifth Form, and Josh was not good at math. For Larry Dunlap, who was good at math, Gilly was a wonderful teacher, but Josh was lost in Gilly's classes. "X" remained an unknown quantity to him. He copied down everything that Gilly wrote on the black-board, but it was a complete mystery when he looked at it later. It took away his appetite to see Gilly at the dinner table.

Still, he did like Oakley most of the time. For one thing, he liked being at an all-boy school. Girls were a pain: a pain in classes, where they always knew all the answers, and a special pain during the past year when dancing instruction had been a part of gym, with the piano going boom, trap, trap, boom, trap, trap. He had hated pushing giggling girls across the gym floor and always stepped on their feet, trying to turn. The only girls here at Oakley were some faculty children, too little to bother him.

As for the strict school schedule, he was getting used to that. He knew where he was supposed to go and how to get there. He no longer got mixed up try-ing to find his classes. He no longer went looking for the elevator that Fifth Formers were told to take. He knew better now. There was no elevator.

14

He liked football and, except for algebra, he liked his classes, especially T.B.'s in ancient history. For their term project the Fifth Form had voted to make maps of the ancient world, putting in as much information as possible. Josh was determined to make the best one in the class. His was so big that he had to lay it on the floor to work on it. He had to keep it under his bed the rest of the time. Larry said it didn't make sense to have it so big.

"You think T.B.'s going to drop dead when he sees it, but he won't. It should be smaller and neater. And it sure is in the way."

Josh knew that this was true, though he would not admit it. In their room there was no safe place for a huge map. They lived next to the mail room and had a window opening onto a porch that connected with South Hall, where most of the classes met. Around noon, when classes were finished, boys would come in to see Larry or Josh while they waited for the mail to be sorted. Sometimes they even came in through the window. With a room full of guys, his map could easily be stepped on or smudged or torn. But Josh thought it was a good room, even if he had to share it with Larry. He was getting to know a lot of guys. Maybe it was just because they lived next to the mail room. Whatever the reason, Josh liked knowing a lot of guys. There were more plebes at Oakley than he had thought there were, and some of the aristos weren't too bad, especially when they were playing football.

15

In the following weeks he liked football more and more. He had always been a fast runner and, with practice every afternoon, he found he could catch a twisting football better than he had ever been able to catch a baseball. His coordination had never been much good, but now it seemed to be improving. Mr. Daily, "the Grind," not only taught Latin but coached the younger boys in football. He told Josh that he might make a good quarterback if he kept at it.

Josh kept at it. He wished he were bigger, like Jerry Loomis, Brillo's roommate, who was a real star, but he probably never would bè very big. Soccer, the other autumn sport, would have brought him fewer bumps and bruises, but he liked football. Learning to tackle the dummy as hard as he could, learning to hold the ball and fall on it, learning the plays—all this was new and exciting. As he trotted back to the locker room with the other players after a good practice, he was warm all over, but with cold clean air in his lungs, and he felt wonderful. The school looked wonderful too. The Lower Field lay along the river, where the maple trees and oaks had all turned red and gold. In the dusk the color burned brighter than ever. Then lights shone out in the clustered buildings of Oakley and the color faded. From the tower of the school chapel, bells were ringing, high, low, chasing each other up and down the scales, their clear notes filling the valley and echoing from the hills. One evening, just as practice was over, the farm truck came by, loaded with apples. Brillo was riding in the back of the truck. He threw an apple to Josh, who caught it in mid-air and ate it while he undressed in the locker room and took his shower. The apple was cold, juicy, and crunchy.

On Wednesday nights the glee club met for practice. Josh liked that almost best of all. The glee club was learning a lot of good songs. One was about a fox who went out on a chilly night. It sounded like what he was seeing as he walked over to the auditorium with Gordon Graham, now known as G.G., and Brillo and Howie Howland. Their feet shuffled through fallen leaves, and their breath made little clouds of steam in the cold air as they tried out the song.

> "The fox went out on a chilly night
> And prayed to the moon to give him light;
> He'd many miles to go that night
> Before he'd reach the town-o."

Later they practiced it again with the whole glee club, forty strong, in the auditorium, under the direction of Swing Lowe. After five or six verses the fox "got back to his nice warm den" and Swing led them into a spiritual.

> "Sometimes I feel like a motherless child,
> A long way from home."

For a moment Josh felt a slight pang under the mournful harmony, but he was not homesick, not really. Not like some of the Fifth Form "brats," who wrote or even telephoned home every night. Josh was glad he had gone to Camp Buddy and knew how to take care of himself.

"That wasn't bad," said Swing. "Only remember to

17

hold onto that last 'ho-o-o-me.' Now we're going to try a new one. This is another spiritual and I think you'll like it—'Joshua Fit the Battle of Jericho.'"

Brillo, sitting next to Josh, nudged him, and a couple of other boys turned to look at him and grin. Swing passed out the words of the new song and played it for them on the piano. It started with some thumping chords in a minor key, boom-boom-boom-boom, boom-boom-boom-boom.

> "Joshua fit the battle of Jericho, Jericho, Jericho;
> Joshua fit the battle of Jericho
> And the walls came tumbling down.

> "You may talk about your Gideon,
> Talk about your men of Saul,
> There's none like good old Josh
> At the battle of Jericho."

Josh thought he would like to try it on his guitar, which was stored in the broom closet across from his room. He had not had time to play since school started. His guitar was a relic of home, where there were hours and hours of free time to sit and strum and life was free and easy.

Swing laid down his baton and said, "That will be all for tonight. You could be worse, but we have a lot to do before the glee-club concert in the spring. It's a joint concert again with Fairfield, like last year."

The upper-form boys whistled and clapped and stamped.

"What's Fairfield?" Josh asked Howie Howland, who passed the question along their row of seats and eventually got an answer. "It's a girls' school, up the river."

"Oh," said Josh. He was not impressed, but he clapped and stamped because everyone else did.

When he got back to his room after the glee-club rehearsal, he found Larry already in bed, eating a chocolate bar. The wrapper lay on the floor. "Crunchee." It was not a brand carried at the school's supply store. The chocolate smelled awfully good, but Larry did not offer him any. Larry was not a very satisfactory roommate. Josh decided that he liked Brillo much more.

Next day late in the afternoon, when football practice was over, Mr. St. Clair saw Josh going by from the Lower Field, headed toward North Hall, and called out, "Cobb, will you take a message to Mr. McGill's house?" He handed Josh an envelope.

Gilly lived in a house by the river. Josh went the whole way at a trot, pleased to have been picked out for the job. On the riverbank near the house he saw Brillo standing under a big oak tree that leaned out over the water. He was looking up into its branches.

"Hey," said Josh.

"Hey," Brillo answered, then added, "Good tree to climb."

"Not now," Josh said. "I'm taking a message to Gilly."

"I like to climb," Brillo said. "In North Hall I can climb up inside the walls and come out in the attic. Some of the walls have sections that come out for plumbing and electric repairs and stuff. I know, because there's one in my room. Nobody else knows. Don't tell."

Josh promised.

Outside the small clapboard house, Mrs. Gilly was raking leaves in the garden. A cream-colored dog with long hair stopped rolling in the leaves and came to sniff at the boys.

"Hello," said Mrs. Gilly. "If you're looking for my husband, I think he's gone up to the chapel."

"We have a message for him," Josh said. "It's from Mr. St. Clair." He held out the envelope.

"Better leave it here," she said. "But if you have time, you might just run up to the chapel and tell him you've left it with me. Here, Winston. Stay."

The cream-colored dog looked back over his shoulder to let her know he had heard, but he followed the two boys.

"Go on back," Josh said. And when they were out of Mrs. McGill's hearing—"Dumb dog." They waved and shouted and threw clods of earth, but Winston trotted after them, unperturbed, up the hill to the chapel. Mr. McGill was nowhere to be seen, even though they walked all the way around the chapel. It seemed to be locked up tight, until they came to the bell tower. Brillo tried the door and it opened. They went in. Winston sat down at the door and watched them go.

"Mr. McGill!" Josh's voice echoed in the empty darkness. Brillo switched on the light.

Josh saw a square room, unfurnished except for two wooden benches and some bronze tablets on the bare plaster walls. In one corner was a flight of stone steps.

"Let's go up," Brillo said. Again he led the way and Josh followed with an uneasy feeling that the school rules said something about the bell tower. Into the room above, the light of the setting sun was pouring through a great window to the west. The golden light lay like a warm carpet on the cold stone floor. From another window to the east, they saw the whole school below them, the pink buildings rising among the trees, the playing fields, the bright thread of the river running between its dark banks, the distant roofs and spires of the town.

When their eyes were accustomed to the brightness, they looked at the room itself. Around the walls were eight small wooden posts. On each post was a loop of rope like a noose. Above the noose was a velvet hand-grip, and above that each rope traveled up through a hole in the ceiling. In one corner an iron ladder led up through a trap door to whatever was above.

"Let's go and see," Brillo said. He scrambled up the ladder, paused with only his feet in view, and let out a whistle. "Come on up," he said, and his feet disappeared.

The ladder was freezing cold to Josh's hands. He went up slowly, his heart beating fast. The top of the ladder ended at a ledge that ran around the highest chamber of the bell tower. Here the light came through wooden slats in the stone walls. Heavy beams crisscrossed above his head, supporting the eight bells. Josh saw with surprise that the bells were upside down in their wooden frames. Beside each bell was a metal wheel. The upper ends of the ropes were lashed to spokes of the wheels and ran in grooves around the rims, then downward through the ceiling holes. Looking upward, Josh sensed the weight and power of the dark bells. He shivered and felt dizzy.

Brillo pointed. "There's one more ladder, See, you can get right up on the beams."

"What for?" Josh quavered.

"To fix the bells, I guess. I want to see what it's like up there. Come on."

"Not me," said Josh. "I'll wait for you down below." He backed down the ladder faster than he had gone up. If Brillo wanted to climb higher, he would have to do it alone.

Brillo's voice echoed from above. "Pull a rope. I want to see what happens."

"Which one?" Josh called dubiously.

"Any one. It doesn't matter which," came the voice.

Cautiously, Josh lifted one of the ropes from its mooring post. He let it swing until it hung straight beneath its ceiling hole. Then he reached up to the velvet handgrip and pulled downward with both hands. A second later, still clinging to the rope in horrified surprise, he was being pulled up toward the ceiling as if a giant had the rope in an iron grip.

From the bell chamber above came a deep *bom,* and again *bom,* as the rope came down. Josh came down with it, letting go of the rope as his feet touched the floor. The rope whipped upward like an angry snake.

Another shock followed. When the room stopped swimming before Josh's eyes, he saw Mr. McGill standing before him with the dog Winston at his side. Winston was panting slightly and appeared to be smiling.

In a terrible voice Mr. McGill asked, "What do you think you're doing, Cobb?"

"I don't know, sir," Josh said faintly.

From the trapdoor Brillo's face looked down, white and scared. "It was my idea, sir."

"Don't get another idea like this one," Mr. McGill said. "No one touches the ropes except the bell ringers, and never—*never,* you understand—when someone is up there with the bells. How would you like to be hit by several hundred pounds of swinging bell? You're both on detention."

With every week that passed at Oakley, Josh was finding that there were a lot of ways to get into trouble at this school.

3

"Fall," Josh said with disgust. "They sure named it right—fall." Because of their adventure in the bell tower, he and Brillo had been on detention for three days, raking the fallen leaves every afternoon with the rest of the detention squad. There were piles of leaves, hills of leaves, mountains of leaves to rake, enough for the biggest detention squad in the world.

Brillo did not care. He said he would just as soon rake leaves as pitch hay and manure in the school barns, his regular activity during the sports period.

But Josh was missing football practice while he raked leaves. As a result, his name was not on the list when Mr. Daily, "the Grind," read out the names of the boys who would play in the last game of the junior football series.

"For those who will not be playing this afternoon," Mr. Daily said, folding up his list, "better luck next time. And don't forget," he added with a faint grin, "some can pass footballs, some can pass exams."

Exams were among the important events that took place at Oakley School toward the end of November. Other events would be class elections, the varsity game against Newton, and the appearance of mid-term grades.

Meanwhile, Josh was still working on his map of the ancient world. All through November he worked on it in every spare minute. Larry's small, neat map was finished and safe in his desk drawer. Brillo said he had not even started his and was trying to think of a good idea, something different.

One night, just before "lights out," Josh was kneeling with his map spread out on the floor. He had his countries and oceans and seas all drawn in and was printing information in little squeezed-up letters around the edges, using every inch of space because T.B. had said to put in as much information as possible. Suddenly Larry opened the door and came in, joggling Josh's arm as he stepped over the map to get to his desk. He was eating a chocolate bar and dropped the wrapper on the map. The label read "Crunchee."

"Look out, will you?" Josh said. "See what you made me do? I made a messy line." He brushed off the candy wrapper, which left a brown smear.

"Sorry about that," said Larry, and again he did not sound sorry. He picked up the wrapper and threw it into the wastebasket. Then he retrieved the paper, tore it into little pieces, and mixed them into the other contents of the basket with rather elaborate care. Josh pushed his finished map out of sight, and a moment later when the bell rang, they were in their beds with lights out. A tantalizing smell of chocolate came from Larry's side of the room.

"Where do you get those Crunchee bars?" Josh asked in the darkness. All he got for an answer was, "Don't you wish you knew?"

He lay awake for a while feeling mad and then slept fitfully. The next day he remembered thinking that he had seen Larry climbing in through the window during the night. It must have been a dream, though it seemed very real. Josh was too busy to think much about it. He handed in his map to T.B., and he also made a special report in Bible Studies, on which he had been working hard. Mr. St. Clair taught that subject to the Fifth Form. Every boy in the class with the name of a Bible hero was to tell the story of the hero to the class. There was no Abraham or Noah or Moses in the Fifth Form, but David Upson had to tell about David and Goliath. Daniel Garrett told about Daniel in the lion's den. Joseph Barry told about Joseph and his brothers. And today Joshua

Cobb was scheduled to tell about Joshua and the walls of Jericho.

Knowing the song, Josh had been curious about the story, which he had never read. When he looked it up in the Old Testament, he thought it was great; and when Mr. St. Clair called on him to tell it, he was all set.

"Well, after the Jews left Egypt, they wanted to get to the Promised Land. So they came to a city called Jericho, with big high walls around it, and some of their enemies lived inside. So God told Joshua he had to take Jericho. Well, some spies snuck in and they got a woman to help them, because I guess she didn't like the enemies much. But first they —the Jews, I mean—had to get across the river Jordan, and it was flooding; but they found some big stones and they came on across. Well, Joshua wondered how he could take Jericho, because they didn't have any good weapons. But God told Joshua not to worry. He said they should march around and around the city for seven days blowing trumpets, and the last day they should blow louder than ever and all shout together and the walls would come tumbling down, and they did." Josh stopped, out of breath, and sat down.

"Very good," Mr. St. Clair said. "I might point out just one or two things. God did not tell Joshua not to worry. He told him to be strong and of good courage. He told him that several times. Joshua still probably had to worry. Almost every leader does. But he

29

could also be strong and of good courage. By the way, there is no such word as 'snuck.' "

Mr. St. Clair then asked for some class discussion. Howie Howland said he did not believe you could make stone walls fall down by blowing trumpets and shouting. G.G. Graham said that a sonic boom could break windows. Mr. St. Clair asked what they knew about psychological warfare, and when the class ended, everyone was talking about different kinds of weapons, from cavemen's clubs to the atomic bomb. Dan Garrett said he had found an Indian arrowhead in the potato field, and he pulled it out of his pocket as proof. It was a good class. The Saint's classes were always pretty good, because he always made everyone talk.

That night the Fifth Form held a meeting to vote for class officers, who would be in power until the spring term. As Josh had suspected, Mead Balfour, Denny Cheswick, Van Stevens, and Larry Dunlap were elected. They were all aristos. But to Josh's surprise, several plebes were also nominated, including Howie Howland and Dan Garrett, both of whom lost by only a narrow margin. Josh voted for Howie and Dan. He also voted for Mead and for Larry. After all, Larry was his roommate, and it did not seem to matter much now whether you were an aristo or a plebe. You knew whom you liked, and you could guess who would make a good class officer. Josh did not really like Larry, but he thought his roommate would make a good class officer. Larry had a lot of savvy. Besides, it would seem bad not to vote for your own room-mate.

As treasurer, Larry went about his job efficiently. By the next day he had a complete list of names for the whole class and collected fifty cents in dues from almost everyone, putting a check mark by each name and adding up the money with speed and ease before depositing it in the school bank. Josh could not help feeling proud to be the roommate of a class officer with so much savvy.

This was the last Saturday in November, the day of the varsity football game against Newton. Oakley had not won a game against Newton for six years. The upper forms did not think they could do it this year either, but the Oakley bleachers, on one side of the Upper Field, were full, and cheering never stopped from the moment of the kickoff. Josh found Larry sitting beside him in the Fifth Form section, yelling his head off, and he knew that Larry felt the way he felt whenever Oakley scored or Newton fumbled. At the half, they were standing together for the school song, sung to the tune of "Maryland, My Maryland":

"Above the river flowing free
Stands Oakley School, our Oakley School.
We pledge our faith and loyalty
To Oakley School, our Oakley School.
Yes, we will all be true to thee
However long the years may be,
Still bright and fair in memory,
Oakley School, our Oakley School."

31

At the end of the fourth quarter, Oakley made a final rally and Alan Crane at quarterback ran for a touchdown, to tie the score. Pandemonium broke loose in the Oakley bleachers, drowning out the answering yells from the Newton ranks across the field. In the breathless pause that followed, Crane kicked the point after touchdown, winning the game for Oakley. Larry and Josh pounded each other's backs, shouting till they were hoarse and their voices were part of one great roar.

But some of Josh's old jealous feeling came back on Monday when T.B. returned their maps of the ancient world. Larry got an A. Josh, who had worked much harder, got a B and a note saying, "This represents a lot of work, but it could be neater." Brillo was in worse trouble. He had not yet turned in his map. He told T.B. that he was working out something entirely new and different for which he needed extra time. T.B. said that Brillo's map had better be turned in at once, no matter how new and different it was, or he would get a very low mark indeed. Term grades appeared, and Brillo had several very low marks. His work was good, but it was almost always late. He told Josh it was not fair.

When the honor roll was read out at Assembly, Larry and Josh were both on it. Josh wrote home to tell his mother the good news. And the best of it was that everyone on the honor roll was allowed to go into town to the Tuck Shop after dinner that night. For most of them it would be their first glimpse of the bright lights since school began.

It was starting to snow as they crossed the bridge. A long column of boys, shouting, laughing, leaning against the wind, hurried toward the lights of the Tuck Shop, which shone out on the main street of the little town. Josh followed the others who were crowding through the door and lining up three deep at the counter. It was warm in the Tuck Shop and the air was thick with the smell of chocolate. Waiting for his turn to order, Josh read the signs on the wall behind the counter.

SUNDAES   SHAKES   SODAS

MOHICAN SPECIAL . . . THREE MARSHMALLOW-COVERED CHOCOLATE ICE CREAM MOUNTAINS WITH A RICH CHOCOLATE SYRUP RIVER RUNNING ROUND THEM. LOADED WITH NUTS AND CHOCOLATE NUGGETS

BRIDGE BANANA SPLIT . . . THE LONGEST SPAN OF GOODNESS IN TOWN. CHOCOLATE, STRAWBERRY, AND VANILLA ICE CREAM TOPPED WITH CHOCOLATE, STRAWBERRY, AND PINEAPPLE SYRUP. A BANANA BRIDGE RISES ABOVE THE DRIFTS OF SNOWY WHIPPED CREAM

Josh's brain reeled and his eyes glazed over. How to choose? At last he settled on a Mohican Special, gave his order, and watched greedily while the counterboy constructed a monumental sundae which fulfilled every promise of the advertisement. Josh finished it off in silent bliss, down to the last scraping of sauce. Since September he had consumed nothing but school food and the second-rate offerings of the candy counter in the supply store. Now every memory of that Spartan fare was canceled out by one Mohican Special.

He turned away, full and satisfied. The crowd was starting to thin out, heading back toward school. Then Josh saw Larry, buying candy. Josh saw the woman behind the candy counter smiling and heard her say, "Hello again. Same as usual?" Larry nodded and the woman handed him a Crunchee bar. Larry paid for it and put it in his pocket.

So this was where Larry got his candy. He must have been coming into town without permission ever since school began. Larry, playing it cool! Without waiting for his roommate, Josh pushed open the door of the Tuck Shop and joined the others, walking fast to keep warm. Somewhere down the road he heard voices singing,

> "The fox went out on a chilly night
> And prayed to the moon to give him light;
> He'd many miles to go that night
> Before he'd reach the town-o."

It was G.G. Graham and Howie Howland. They seemed to be feeling fine. But Josh was not feeling fine. His stomach was vaguely uncomfortable, and he was not sure why. It might have been caused by too much Mohican Special or it might be the unpleasant suspicion that Larry was heading toward real trouble.

34

Against the dark sky, the crisscross girders of the bridge were white with new-fallen snow. Beyond the bridge were two yellow patches where lamps glowed in the windows of Gilly's house. Suddenly a cream-colored form appeared at Josh's feet and Winston launched himself upward, all soppy paws and wet hair.

"Down, you dumb dog," Josh said, fending off Winston with one hand and mopping at his trousers and jacket with the other.

The door of Gilly's house opened. Mrs. Gilly stood there whistling and calling, "Winston! Here, Winston! Home, boy."

Winston stood still for a moment, listening. Then he trotted after Josh's retreating figure.

"That dog must like you," said G.G.

"I wish he didn't," Josh said. "He gives me a pain."

Winston followed them to the door of North Hall. When the door closed in his face, he sat down disconsolately in the snow. He waited until Larry, the last straggler, returned from town, eating a candy bar. Then he went home.

4

"This roommate of yours," said Dusty. "Is he a good guy?"

"I don't know. I guess so," Josh answered. They had just finished eating Christmas dinner and had helped to clear the table. Josh's mother had refused further help and closed herself in the kitchen to wash the dishes in peace.

Josh lay on the rug in front of the fire, and Dusty filled the biggest chair, his long legs stretched out in a new pair of civilian trousers. Dusty was Josh's favorite counselor from his two summers at camp and was a good substitute for the older brother Josh would like to have had. And, since Dusty had no family of his own, the Cobbs' home was a substitute for the one *he* would like to have had. Now on Christmas leave from the Marine Corps, he felt especially good relaxing with Josh and his mother.

"I mean, what is he like?" Dusty persisted.

"Larry? Gee, I can hardly remember," Josh said. "He's smart, though, and he plays it cool all the time." Then he added, "School seems so far away." It seemed not only far away but unreal. Now, for two whole weeks at home, his days had been blissfully empty except for what he wanted to put into them. Home! Sleeping as late as you like. Regal breakfasts! "What would you like this morning, dear?" Sausages and waffles swimming in syrup. Sauntering out to buy a few Christmas presents and wrapping them at leisure. Looking up old friends for a movie or a professional hockey game. And then the arrival of Dusty, friendly as ever, taller, with broader, straighter shoulders, but still the same Dusty who had played the ukulele at camp and who was always easy to talk to and always on your side.

"Do you still play your uke?" Josh asked.

"Not since I went into the Marines," Dusty said. "There hasn't been any time."

"Not for me either," said Josh. "My guitar is in the broom closet at school. I haven't touched it once. I talked about it to Ali Baba—that's Ali Mahmud—

and Scotty Scott. Ali's father might send him an instrument you hold with your feet, and Scotty is learning the saxophone. We were going to have a happening."

"Maybe you'll have it when you go back."

"There still won't be time. I'll have too much work to do. The winter term is supposed to be the hardest one. And I want to play hockey. T. B. Bishop coaches it and I like him. There's skiing and basketball and hockey in the winter term, but I'm not tall enough for basketball and I can't ski."

"Can you skate?"

"Not very well. I still fall down a lot."

"Then try out for goalie," Dusty advised.

Talking about school made it seem more real and also gave Josh his first chance to get some things off his chest. He told Dusty about having to run a mile if you were late for breakfast. He told him about Job Assembly and the detention squad, and about a few First Formers whom he disliked and feared.

"You'll find a few guys like that wherever you go," said Dusty. "Same in the Marines."

"And you can break a rule without even knowing you did it."

"Well, as long as you don't know you're breaking one—" Dusty began.

But Josh shook his head. "Ignorance of the law is no excuse. That's what they say at Oakley."

"Same in the Marines," Dusty said.

Suddenly Josh burst out with something he had

never told anyone. "Larry goes to town all the time without permission. I would never have the nerve."

"What happens if you do?"

"I don't know," Josh said. "It's not as bad as smoking, but it's bad."

"Well, don't be a stoolie," Dusty advised him. "It's not your business what he does. If he's so smart, he must know what he's doing. But then some people can be smart and still be stupid."

"I know, but I sort of like him," Josh said. "At first I didn't, but now I do." A vivid picture of Larry flashed into his mind and he said, "Larry's a class officer." Out of the corner of his eye he tried to see whether Dusty was impressed, but it was hard to tell. Then he thought about his new Oakley blazer, a Christmas present hanging in the closet, ready for the return to school. "I want to get started on the winter term," he said.

That mood passed, but until the end of vacation he went on telling Dusty about Oakley, about the river, about Brillo and the bell tower, and about football, and the glee club, and the classes that he liked best. Dusty was interested in the story about Joshua and the walls of Jericho, and he was glad that Josh was on the honor roll.

"Brillo would be on it too—he's a lot smarter than I am, but he never gets his stuff in on time," Josh said.

"That's what I mean," said Dusty. "Some guys are smart but dumb. You'll do all right the way you are.

Just keep going and be yourself. It sounds O.K., though, at Oakley," he added thoughtfully. "If I ever make it through college, I wouldn't mind teaching there some day."

Much too soon it was New Year's and Dusty's leave was over. Until now, Josh had felt half asleep, drifting through the long, lazy vacation days, but all at once time began to pass like water rushing over a dam. He hurried through his last breakfast at home, slammed the lid of his tightly packed suitcase, and kissed his mother goodbye. Then he made a wild dash for the bus station, and the wheels were turning, carrying him away from a comfortable home, carrying him back to Oakley for the winter term. He supposed it would be tough.

By the time the bus stopped at Oakley in the late afternoon, it was full of boys who had boarded it at various points. The snow was piled in deep drifts along the road. Between the town and the school the white expanse was unbroken except where the black branches of bare trees marked the edges of the Mohican. The river was frozen solid and the wind had swept the ice clean. Ahead, Josh saw Dan Garrett and Brillo. He caught up with them and they crossed the bridge together just as a solitary skater sped under it —Swing Lowe, executing a stylish turn and raising a mittened hand in salute.

"Wash your face, brush your teeth, comb your hair," Brillo said under his breath.

Josh grinned. They were back all right.

40

Larry returned later by car, almost late for dinner. He said that he had had a rotten time, having spent his entire Christmas vacation in the dentist's chair. His face was broken out. "Christmas candy," he explained. He had a pair of skis and said he would try them out on the slopes for advanced skiers.

The next day in English class Swing Lowe started them on the *Iliad* and the *Odyssey*. He was so full of enthusiasm that he began talking before he had even reached his desk.

"We will spend the winter term reading parts of these two great books," he said. "Most of you already know about the wooden horse which the Greeks used to trick the Trojans and win their ten years' war. You know that Achilles was the greatest Greek fighter and Ulysses the cleverest one. We will be reading about the heroic battles of Achilles and about Ulysses' long journey home from the war. These stories are thousands of years old, but they are still exciting today. Someone has said that the *Iliad* is great because life is a battle, and the *Odyssey* is great because life is a journey. Do you think that is true?"

Josh thought it was true, but he could not put his feeling into words. Swing looked over the faces of the silent class. "No one seems to want to tackle that question. I think I am seeing the aftereffects of Christmas vacation. What about 'Merrily, merrily, life is but a dream'? Does that represent your sentiments?"

The class stirred fitfully.

"Or perhaps 'Life is just a bowl of cherries'? But,

41

no. That song belongs to an earlier generation. Well, let us set the scene for the *Iliad*." Flipping through the pages, Swing found the place he wanted and launched forth, pacing up and down, his eyes gleaming. "Vulcan, you see, made a wonderful shield for Achilles. The shield was round and made of silver and gold. On it he made a design showing the whole world as Homer knew it—lands and seas, sun, moon and stars, busy cities, young men and girls dancing, farms, pastures, and animals, vineyards, all the work men did. And around the edge of the shield he showed Ocean circling the earth. You will find this description in Book Eighteen. Read it first and you will have a perfect picture of the ancient world. . . . Would anyone care to comment? No comments? Any questions?" Mr. Lowe's face brightened. "Ah, Brilovich has a question. What is your question, Brilovich?"

"When can we read *Catcher in the Rye,* sir?"

Mr. Lowe looked hurt. "Today, if you like," he said impatiently. "Get it at the library, by all means. I suppose you will think it bears a close resemblance to your life here at Oakley. Now, back to the *Iliad* and the *Odyssey*. You will write a term paper, due at the end of February, on this subject: Are the *Iliad* and the *Odyssey* relevant to our life today? Style will count, as well as your ideas. And watch your spelling. I will take five points off your grade for each misspelling."

On the way out of the classroom Josh asked Brillo, "What's this *Catcher in the Rye?*"

42

"It's a neat book," said Brillo, "about a guy at school. He goes nutty. Actually, I've already read it. I just wanted to hear what old Swing would say."

For the next two weeks Josh did not see much of Brillo. His manner was friendly but vague when they did meet. Brillo belonged to the science club, which was designing space rockets. Maybe that was why he looked as if he were involved in some private project thousands of miles away.

Josh was busy too. He had signed up for hockey, which demanded every extra minute. Following Dusty's advice, he tried out for goalie. It looked like the easiest position, but the facts proved otherwise. True, the goalie did not need the same kind of skill with the hockey stick and skates demanded by the other positions. But the goalie needed special skills and had his own special problems. He had to get used to the enormous leg guards that made him waddle like a robot. And it was no picnic to keep a tense, lonely vigil in front of the cage while his team slashed and scrambled far away in enemy territory. Sooner or later they would come, the whole field veering and swooping down on him with fury, driving the puck before them at a hundred miles an hour. To stop that puck was like stopping a bullet. Not to stop it was worse. So, stop it! with stick or skates or with your whole body flung on the ice to protect the goal. At night he dreamed of defending his goal. In his dreams he was tiny, and a speeding horde of giants rushed toward him with a dozen pucks.

But in his waking hours he knew he was not doing

too badly, and when the next issue of the school paper came out, he wrote to his mother, "Here is something about hockey that I cut out of the *Oakley Oracle*. Be sure to read the last sentence." It read, "Fifth Former Josh Cobb shows promise at goalie for the junior team." Josh added in his letter, "I'm glad I'm not on detention. The detention squad has to flood the rink at night and it's supposed to be the coldest job there is."

The very next day Brillo met Josh in the corridor of North Hall and said mysteriously, "I've got something to show you. Come on." He led the way to his room on the second floor. Jerry Loomis, Brillo's roommate, was in the infirmary with mumps, so they had the room to themselves. Brillo closed the door and pushed the dresser against it. Then he produced a screw driver from a dresser drawer and went to work on a panel in the wall, where his dresser had stood. Quickly removing two loose screws, he lifted out the wooden panel, exposing a narrow passage filled with metal pipes.

"This way," whispered Brillo. "But look out. Some of the pipes are hot." He clambered upward, touching each pipe experimentally before using it to hoist himself into the space above. With a fleeting memory of the bell tower, Josh followed, wondering where the climb would lead this time. A moment later he found out. They were in the attic above Brillo's room. In the center of the room and bolted to the floor were two lines of low wooden seats, each supplied with a handle. Josh guessed these to be rowing machines for early crew practice. Near one window the floor was covered with newspaper, paint pots, scissors and glue, the purpose of which he could not guess. But most of all Josh noticed a litter of cigarette stubs.

Under his breath he asked, "Did you smoke all of these?"

Brillo shrugged. "Not all of them. A lot of guys must have been up here before me." But he had not come to show Josh a place for secret smoking. He lifted a piece of newspaper and said, "Look."

On the floor lay a circle of gold and silver as big as a cartwheel. It shone in the light that came through the window. Josh recognized it at once—the shield of Achilles.

5

"You mean you made it?" he said. "Gosh, it must have been hard work."

"It was," Brillo agreed. "And it's not finished. I want to make it exactly right. I can't get in everything Homer said, but I'm doing all I can."

He pulled a battered paperback copy of the *Iliad* from his trousers pocket and read, " 'First he shaped the shield so great and strong, adorning it all over and binding it round with a gleaming circuit in three layers.' " Brillo pointed. "See, mine is three layers around the edge."

"Three layers of what?"

"Cardboard," said Brillo. "And his was five thicknesses in the middle, and so is mine." He went on reading, " '. . . the earth, the heavens, and the sea; the moon also at her full and the untiring sun, with all the signs that glorify the face of heaven—' That's the signs of the zodiac. I've made them too, see?"

Josh was lost in wonder and admiration, while Brillo went on reading and pointing out the details of the shield he had made according to the description in the book. " 'He wrought also a vineyard, golden and fair to see, and the vines were loaded with grapes. The bunches overhead were black, but the vines were trained on poles of silver.' "

"Here it is," said Josh, finding Brillo's vineyard. "But what are you going to do with it—hand it in to Swing Lowe?"

"No," said Brillo. "It's for T.B. Bishop. It's my map of the ancient world. I told him I was going to make something special for that map assignment, and I have."

"But it isn't a map," Josh said doubtfully, when they were back in Brillo's room with the wall panel and the dresser replaced.

"What do you mean, it isn't a map?" said Brillo, looking stubborn. "It's a perfect map, just the way Homer would have made it, and it has a lot of information. T.B. had better like it."

"Well, I think it's great," Josh said hastily. "You must be a genius or something."

The following day was clear, cold, and bright, with snow sparkling under sun and blue sky. Everyone else, except for a few victims of the mumps, had gone to skate on the river. Josh and Brillo had North Hall to themselves. They went up into the attic again. Brillo uncovered the shield to add a few finishing touches. He consulted his book and read, " 'All round the outermost rim of the shield he set the mighty stream of the river Oceanus.' " He dipped a brush into a bottle of gold paint and set to work. Then he reached into his shirt pocket and took out a pack of cigarettes.

"I work better if I smoke," he said. "Have one?"

With a sudden resolve, Josh took a cigarette from the hand of the genius. They sat on the floor smoking while Brillo finished painting the mighty stream of the river Oceanus. The attic was sunny and quiet. Below them Josh could hear shouts from skaters on the Mohican. He heard a dog barking.

"Better open the window a little in case someone comes back and smells smoke," said Brillo. "The door is always locked, but someone must have a key."

Josh went to the window, unlatched it, and pushed it open slightly. Then he looked down. Mr. and Mrs. McGill were skating past, hand in hand. Winston was standing on the riverbank, barking. When the window creaked open, Winston cocked his head and seemed to listen. Then he trotted to the wall of North Hall and looked up at the attic.

"That dumb dog," said Josh, ducking down. "I

50

think he saw me. And Gilly just went past. He looked up when Winston came barking."

Winston began to bark again, louder. Little curls of smoke were floating through the open window.

"Did Gilly see anything?" asked Brillo.

"I don't know," Josh said nervously.

"Close the window," Brillo told him. "Stub out your cigarette and let's go. Get your skates and we'll head for the river before anyone comes looking. Help me carry this stuff down."

Ten minutes later, mingling with other skaters, they headed upriver.

Josh said, "I still smell of smoke."

"Only inside yourself. No one else can smell you now."

They skated on in silence until the other Oakley skaters were left behind. The sun began to set. To the east the snowy hilltops turned gold. Purple shadows covered the lower slopes. Suddenly, around a bend, they saw a bonfire blazing on the darkened west bank of the river, smoke streaming out from the flames. A record player was broadcasting dance music and some girls skated past, circled around Josh and Brillo, and headed back toward the bonfire. The whole river was full of skating girls.

"Let's go back," Josh said. He spun around and collided with a skater in a red cap and red jacket. Pushing clear with both hands, he had only time to see her wide smile, dark eyes, and long brown hair whipped by the wind. Then she was gone.

When he got his breath back he said, "What do you suppose all that was?"

"Must have been Fairfield," Brillo said. "I knew it was up here somewhere. Their glee club is coming down for a rehearsal pretty soon, remember? Not bad."

Josh wondered if the girl with the smile was in the Fairfield glee club. She had to be.

The sun set as they skated back toward Oakley. Lights shone warmly from houses along the river. A peal of bells from the chapel tower chimed in the distance, and from under their feet sounded the hiss of steel blades cutting smooth ice. With the wind at their backs, Josh and Brillo sped downriver toward Oakley. Smoking in the attic was no longer the main event of the day just past. For Josh, that adventure was eclipsed by one moment on the ice at Fairfield, when he had heard music, seen a bonfire, and bumped into a girl. In the night he dreamed again that he was guarding his cage on the hockey rink, but now he was as big as a First Former, and the rink was empty except for himself and a girl who came skimming toward him, beautifully balanced on one skate, leaning forward, head up, arms stretched out like a bird's wings.

At Job Assembly the next morning, that dream seemed about to come true when Alan Crane announced, "On the last Saturday in January, the Fairfield glee club will come down for a rehearsal of the spring concert. There will be a junior hockey game

that afternoon, if we can round up a couple of teams. Volunteers should speak to the coach. There will also be a small dance after the rehearsal. Members of the Oakley glee club can attend if they want to." Here he was interrupted by cheers, clapping, stamping of feet, and general laughter. Crane went on, "Class officers of all forms can attend the dance too. It will be called the Snow Ball and there will be decorations which the detention squad can make. Mr. Marvell has the stuff."

Crane's next announcement was no dream. It was reality, and grim. Sounding like a top sergeant, he said that Mr. McGill had seen someone at the window of the North Hall attic and wanted to say something about it.

Gilly stood up in his place and began impressively, looking from face to face. "Thanks, Crane. This is something that I want to make very clear. I thought I recognized a face at the attic window, but I'm not sure. As you all know, that attic door is kept locked, but someone had come up through a space between the walls. He had been painting. When I went up to investigate, I found cigarette stubs all over the floor, also newspapers. I don't know why the building hasn't burned down. If you are bright enough to be in this school, you are bright enough to understand why there is a rule against smoking, so I will not spell out the reasons. The point is, from now on, any boy found smoking will be suspended. Period." Mr. McGill sat down.

Suspended! Josh's stomach felt as if he had swallowed a hockey puck. On the way out of Job Assembly he avoided Brillo, and he did not answer when Larry said cheerfully, "Old Gilly really lowered the boom, didn't he?"

Josh was still sunk in gloom when he went into T.B. Bishop's class, and he broke out in a cold sweat when he saw the shield of Achilles propped up against the blackboard. He noticed that Brillo was looking tense.

T.B. said nothing about the shield until he had led the class through a discussion of the Punic Wars and told the story of Hannibal crossing the Alps. Then he said, "During this class period you have all had a chance to look at the shield which Brilovich has just handed in. He says it is a map of the ancient world, for the assignment that was due two months ago. I confess I am stumped. Brilovich has done a fine job, an outstanding job. But it is . . . offbeat, for a map, to say the least, and it is very late. Brilovich has suggested that we put it to a class vote, since it was a class decision to make maps in the first place. Shall I accept this shield as a map of the ancient world? Write yes or no on a piece of paper and hand it in as you leave."

Josh voted yes, but he did not have much hope for Brillo's chances. Scotty Scott said, shaking his head as they left the room, "That guy is a real oddball."

"I don't care if he is a nut," said G.G. Graham. "I wish I had made that shield, or even thought of it. But, two months late! That's too much."

56

As Josh expected, the vote went against Brillo. T.B. announced the results the following day in class. "Brilovich, six voted to accept your work as a map. Ten voted no. So I regret to tell you that you still have to make a map. However, Brilovich, I am putting the shield of Achilles on display in the library with a copy of the *Iliad* open at the proper page."

Josh thought the vote was fair, but he felt bad about the way it had turned out. Brillo did not seem to care about the vote.

"They're a bunch of chumps anyway, and I can make a regular map in nothing flat," he said, adding with satisfaction, "T.B. put my shield in the big display case. It looks really great. Everyone is going in to look at it. Want to see it?"

Josh followed Brillo into the school library. Mr. McGill was standing in front of the big display case, looking at the shield.

"Ah, there, Brilovich," he said. "I believe this is your work? Very good. Silver and gold over cardboard—it's effective. One question, Brilovich. The paint I found on the attic floor was silver and gold. There were some scraps of cardboard. Please see me in my office after lunch."

Josh did not eat much lunch. He saw Brillo leave the dining hall, and he followed when Brillo headed for Gilly's office. It might not be a wise move, but he could not help hanging around that office door until Brillo came out. At last he reappeared. Josh joined him and they moved off together, walking quickly.

"What did he say?" Josh asked.

"He wanted to know if I was smoking, and I said yes. He put me on probation."

"What does that mean?"

"No privileges for the rest of the year. I can't go to the glee-club dance, for one thing. He said if he caught me smoking again, I'd be suspended. And if I do it and he doesn't catch me, I'm supposed to turn myself in. It's a trap, either way."

"Does he know about me?"

"Of course not. What do you think I am?"

"Maybe I ought to tell him."

"What for? Don't be dumb."

But Josh could not get the problem off his mind. Brillo was not only a genius, he was a hero. He had made the marvelous shield. He was not afraid to smoke. And he took his punishment alone, protecting a friend. What should that friend do?

6

It snowed all afternoon. When classes were over, the Fifth and Fourth Forms built forts on Chapel Hill and waged a fierce snowball battle, only calling truces when the wounded had to be removed, with black eyes or bloody noses. The snow was still falling when Josh went to bed that night. Larry was already in bed with the covers drawn up under his chin, his eyes closed, and his sharp nose pointed toward the ceiling. Josh turned out the light and dived under his covers, but he had too much on his mind to go to sleep.

He lay awake watching the big white snowflakes that drifted past the window in the dim light of an outside lamp. Presently, Larry's bed creaked. Josh saw him standing up, fully dressed even to his ski jacket and boots. He must have worn them to bed. He stretched himself. Then he stepped quietly to the opened window, raised it higher, and climbed out onto the porch. He lowered the window behind him to an inch from the sill and disappeared into the night. Josh knew what Larry was going to do. He lay still, thinking that he himself would never have enough nerve to do the same thing. He was already in plenty of trouble and didn't need more.

It seemed a long time—he could not tell how long —until Larry returned, raising the window and stepping softly into the room. He closed the window all the way and Josh heard him say "Brr-r-r" under his breath. Then he undressed, leaving his clothes on the floor, and got into bed. A moment later Josh heard the crackle of paper, and a familiar smell of Crunchee chocolate floated across the room.

The next day Josh presented himself at Mr. McGill's office. Gilly was busy at his desk, but he looked up and said pleasantly, "Be with you in a moment, Cobb. I'm correcting papers from the latest efforts of the Fifth Form. Not brilliant."

Josh looked around while he waited. He was too stiff with fright to notice much except three photographs, one of Albert Einstein, one of Mrs. Gilly, and one of Winston.

Mr. McGill put down his pencil, took off his glasses, and leaned back. "Well, Cobb, I assume you have come about simultaneous equations. I thought you were in a fog on that subject, and now that I've read your paper, I know it. Lost, aren't you?"

"Yes, sir," Josh said, examining his shoes. "But I didn't come about that."

"Then what can I do for you?" asked Mr. McGill.

"Nothing, I guess, sir. I came to turn myself in."

"For what?"

"I was smoking with Brillo in the attic." The moment the words were out, he felt better.

Gilly sighed. "I thought I recognized you, but I hoped I was wrong. What a piece of foolishness, Cobb. I shall have to put you on detention for a week."

Josh looked up. Not probation? Only detention? Good old detention, he had been on that half a dozen times and there was nothing to it. Mr. McGill was looking at him in a friendly way.

"I'm glad you came and told me, Cobb. Brilovich did not mention you, of course, and he was quite right. But, while we're on the subject, I think you make a mistake in tagging along after Brilovich all the time. Why do you?"

Josh was surprised. "Because we're friends."

Gilly replaced his glasses and looked piercingly at Josh. "That part is all right. But when I find you in trouble, he seems to have supplied the ideas and you

61

follow. You'll never get anywhere that way, except into his trouble."

On the defensive, Josh said, "He's a great guy."

"Of course he is; one of the greatest. He will go a long way, if I'm not mistaken. He won't have an easy time of it, but that's his style. You have yours, if you only knew it. No two people are exactly alike. Find out who you are, and be that person. As they say these days, do your own thing. Didn't anyone ever suggest that to you?"

In the back of his mind Josh heard Dusty Moore's advice at Christmas time, "Just keep going, and be yourself."

He stood up, ready to lick the world. "Yes, sir. . . . I'm glad it's only detention."

Mr. McGill laughed skeptically. "Maybe you'll change your mind when you've helped the detention squad flood the ice rink a few times. I hope you have a warm jacket. It's a cold job. Also, you might consider skipping the glee-club dance, since Brilovich is on probation and will have to miss it." He ushered Josh out of the office, saying, "Come in again soon and I'll try to explain simultaneous equations."

Josh left, his feeling of relief somewhat modified by the fact that he had not thought about the glee-club dance when he had made up his mind to "turn himself in." And he had not fully considered the prospect of flooding the ice rink, a job which was generally agreed to be the grimmest of the winter term.

On Thursday night before the concert rehearsal, the detention squad flooded the ice. They took turns with four hoses and warmed up between turns in a small shelter beside the rink. The icy water sprayed over them whenever the wind veered. Josh thought about the South Pole and wondered if it could be much colder than this.

On Friday he had a sore throat. He considered reporting to the infirmary but decided against it, since Mrs. Gordon, the school nurse, would undoubtedly rule out Saturday's hockey game the moment she got the thermometer into his mouth.

Friday evening, Brillo took charge of decorations for the dance, and he rounded up the entire Fifth Form in the recreation room. He pointed out a pile of Kleenex boxes and a supply of paper clips.

"Here's the idea," he said. "You fold a couple of Kleenex like this and clip them together in the middle. Then you sort of wad up the whole thing, like this—and it's a snowball."

"Looks like used Kleenex to me," Josh said hoarsely.

"It won't when the time comes. You'll see," Brillo predicted, adding, "Gee, you sound terrible."

"Don't tell anybody," Josh answered, "or they might not let me play tomorrow."

The Fifth Form made a mountain of Kleenex snowballs, while Brillo brought in a clean sheet from his own room and sprayed it liberally with sparkle. Then he turned it over, plain side up, and tied a long piece of fishing line to each corner. On top of the sheet he piled all the Kleenex snowballs and supervised while the whole thing was slung to hang like a sparkling cloud under the rafters.

"Now turn out the center lights," he said, "and we'll see how it's going to look under a spotlight."

In the darkened room, picked out by the spotlight, the great white cloud was an enormous success.

"And," said Brillo, "when the last dance begins, we pull two strings, the corners fall open, and we have a snowstorm."

"That's if everything works right," Josh croaked. "I still think it's going to look like a lot of Kleenex."

But Brillo only said, "Don't argue."

By Saturday Josh could not talk above a whisper, but his throat felt better. He would definitely be able to play in the game. This pleased him, but he paid a price. Since he was the only glee-club member who also played hockey, he was the only member who was not on hand to meet the bus from Fairfield. The officers of each class were also slated to meet the bus, ready to escort the girls on a tour of the school before the hockey game. This meant that Larry would be there. News of the arrival reached the two volunteer teams as they were getting into their uniforms, and Josh wondered if the girl with the big smile was with the Fairfield glee club.

She was. As soon as he came out of the field house onto the rink, he saw her. She was wearing the red cap and jacket and she was standing with Larry Dunlap. Josh skated into position to guard his cage while the teams warmed up. He wondered if she saw him. His cage was pretty far away, and she could probably see every other player better than she could see him. Even if she did see him, maybe she would not recognize him as the one who had bumped into her on the ice at Fairfield.

The whistle blew and Josh put her out of his mind. He had enough to do watching the other players and watching the puck that threatened his cage. If the other team made a goal today, it would be over his dead body. At the end of the period he had held them to no score.

When he skated to the other end of the rink for the second period, he looked for the girl with the red cap, but he could not see her. Maybe she was there somewhere, cheering, but it was hopeless to try to find her in the crowd.

In the second period there was still no score on either side. Returning to his original post for the final period, he heard voices from both sides of the rink. "Good man, Cobb! Attaboy, Cobb! Hold 'em, Cobb!" Well, that girl would know his name even if he did not know hers. Grimly, confidently, Josh settled down to defend his goal. He held it against every attack, and his team, secure in the strength of that defense, launched a slashing assault on the opposing goal, scoring twice before the last whistle. It was a resounding victory.

When Josh left the rink, Brillo was the first person

to slap him on the back. Brillo had a girl with him, a short blond girl with short hair and pink cheeks.

"This is Becky," Brillo said. "We just met. Becky, er—"

"Goodall," she said, smiling and hunching her shoulders against the cold. "Wow, what a game! You were terrific."

She was pretty, but she was not the one he was looking for. His eyes on the departing crowd, he whispered, "Where's Larry?"

"Bad throat," Brillo explained to Becky. Then, "Larry left a long time ago. He took some girl to the ski slopes. I think she's the one who—you know. I'm taking Becky to look at the tadpoles in the science lab. See you later."

Josh went off to change his clothes. So, That Girl had not seen the game at all, or only the beginning, because Larry had taken her away. The glee-club dance was off bounds. That only left supper and the concert rehearsal when he might meet her.

Swing Lowe joined him on his way from the field house to North Hall. "Good game, Cobb. You really held them."

Unwarily, Josh whispered, "Thanks."

Swing looked at him suspiciously. "What's happened to your voice?"

No answer.

"Lost it, eh? You're lucky it's not mumps, but better not try to sing tonight. And get Mrs. Gordon to take a look at you in the morning."

Blast! There went the concert rehearsal. That left

supper. He had better find Larry and try to sit where he sat, in case Larry still had her in tow.

But the girls were scattered all through the crowd in the dining hall when Josh spotted Larry there. Larry was alone. Josh sat down beside him anyway.

"I hear you won," Larry said. "Good show. Sorry I missed most of it. I took a girl to the ski slopes. Borrowed some skis for her and we had a great time. She's the one sitting at the head table."

Now Josh saw her. "What's her name?" he whispered.

"Helen. Helen Crane. She's Crane's sister. I already knew her. I met her at a party last summer."

Helen Crane. Just his luck. If that girl was the sister of Alan Crane, head prefect of Oakley School, he, Joshua Cobb, lowly Fifth Form plebe, might as well try to meet Helen of Troy.

After dinner, Mr. St. Clair made a short speech welcoming the girls from Fairfield. Since tonight's rehearsal was for working purposes, there would be no audience. (Applause and laughter from the combined glee clubs, groans from the uninvited majority of Oakley.) For the spring concert itself, the girls could be sure there would be standing room only, and Oakley would go all-out to give Fairfield a good time. (General applause and cheers.) Another event of the spring-concert weekend would be a meeting of two Oakley debating teams on the following subject: If the Age of Chivalry has departed, it should return. (Deafening cheers.)

Josh had no voice and no heart for applauding. He

could not sing tonight. He would not even hear the rehearsal, since no audience was allowed. And the dance was off bounds for him. He might as well go to bed and forget the whole thing. But as he headed for North Hall, Swing Lowe caught up with him in the yard.

"Cobb, you'd better attend the rehearsal. Even if you can't sing, you can at least learn something by listening."

Slightly cheered, Josh reversed his steps and made for the auditorium, where he ran into Brillo and Becky.

"Stick around for the dance and help us run the record player," said Brillo. "The whole detention squad can help with the dance. Captain Marvell says so." Brillo grinned. "He ain't so bad."

All at once the evening took a turn for the better. Josh sat in the front row of the auditorium during the concert rehearsal. He sat there in solitary splendor where no girl could fail to see him. Helen Crane did not fail to see him, he was sure. She stood right in the middle of the front row of girls.

Oakley sang "Sometimes I Feel like a Motherless Child," and the combined glee clubs sang "The Fox Went Out on a Chilly Night." Oakley followed with "Joshua Fit the Battle of Jericho." When they finished the last verse, Swing Lowe said casually, "By the way, in case the girls are wondering, our audience tonight consists of Joshua Cobb, who held the opposing team to a shutout in the hockey game this afternoon." And suddenly everyone on the stage was clapping. Josh looked at the ceiling, squirmed in his seat, turned cold, turned hot, wished the floor would open up and let him drop into the hole. He did not pull himself together until the next song began.

It proved to be a Fairfield specialty, a medley of TV commercials, which Oakley thought was the best yet. Then the Fairfield accompanist played an introduction for "Coming through the Rye," and the girls sang,

> "If a body meet a body, coming through the rye,
> If a body kiss a body, need a body cry?
> Every lassie has her laddie, nane they say have I,
> Yet all the lads they smile on me when coming
> through the rye."

The second verse brought the high point of the evening for Josh. It was a solo and it was sung by none other than Helen Crane. Her voice was rather low and very clear. Against a background of humming by the Fairfield glee club, she sang,

> "Amang the train there is a swain I dearly love
> mysel',
> But what his name or where his hame I dinna
> choose to tell."

Then came all the girls' voices together again in the refrain,

> "Every lassie has her laddie, nane they say have I,
> Yet all the lads they smile on me when coming
> through the rye."

69

Oakley answered with "There Is Nothing like a Dame," giving it everything they had, but Josh hardly heard it. He wondered if Helen Crane had anybody special in mind when she sang that solo. Anyway, she at least knew his name.

The dance was nothing like the old dances in the school gym at home. Everyone except Josh was having a great time, most of all Larry Dunlap, who came to the dance because he was a class officer. He danced every dance with Helen Crane, and she looked as if she liked him. Brillo was lucky too. Becky stayed with him, helping him to choose the music for the record player. There was not much for Josh to do except pick up Coke bottles and watch the dancing.

Mr. Marvell appeared, wearing a good suit and smiling benevolently on his detention squad. He had been letting his hair grow. It stood up like a bristle brush all over his head.

"Enjoying the detention squad this evening, Cobb?" he asked. "Better than flooding the ice rink, isn't it?" He strolled away.

When the last dance began, Brillo said to Josh, "You take the string in this corner of the room and I'll take the opposite one. When I signal, you pull."

His plan worked not too badly. The lights went out and the spotlight was turned on. To the "Oh's" and "Ah's" of the dancers, the big cloud sparkled overhead. Then Brillo waved to Josh, the strings fell free, and the cloud disgorged a storm of snowballs. Brillo looked as pleased as if he had just opened a new show on Broadway. He was grinning from ear to ear when he set off to take Becky to the bus.

Larry took Helen Crane. As they left, Josh was standing near the door with his hands full of Coke bottles. He heard Larry say, "Corn Cobb." Natch, thought Josh. Natch. It was the same old story—winner, Dunlap; loser, Cobb.

7

In the deep snows of February a midwinter madness descended upon Oakley School. Disturbances broke out repeatedly in Study Hall. Sometimes paper clips were fired across the room from hidden launching pads. Sometimes a subdued humming of TV commercials would begin. Since every mouth was closed and every head was bent industriously above books and papers, the frustrated prefects who monitored Study Hall could never identify the culprits.

Even the First Formers succumbed to the general

72

unrest. One cold day a trio of these mighty ones plugged the drains in a shower-room floor above the dining hall, sealed the door with wet towels, and flooded the floor a foot deep in hot water. They were sitting happily in it when T.B. Bishop came down the corridor in his bathrobe to take a shower. The full wrath of authority fell on the guilty and a large bill for the repair of the dining-hall ceiling was sent to their parents.

It was also during February that someone began setting off the fire alarm by the mail-room door in North Hall after "lights out." Time and again, the peace and quiet was shattered as the gong sounded its raucous warning, forcing everyone to leap out of bed and prepare to evacuate the building. Mr. St. Clair called a special Assembly to discuss the seriousness of the situation, but without effect. Living next to the mail room, Josh and Larry were questioned and found innocent. They were in a favorable position to do some detective work, but their room was cold and their beds were warm. No matter how hard they tried to keep awake, they always fell asleep before the mysterious alarm sounded.

One night Josh heard a sound in the corridor. Like a shot, he flung himself at the door and into the hall. What he saw was Mr. Marvell stepping into the broom closet. Mr. Marvell saw Josh, signaled for silence, and backed into the closet, closing the door on himself. There was a clatter, a thump, and a sound of twanging. Mr. Marvell opened the closet door and thrust a guitar into Josh's hands.

"Get this thing out of here," he mumbled. "I'm going to find out who's ringing that alarm if I have to wait here till hell freezes over." He closed the door again.

That night the phantom did not strike, and the next day Mr. Marvell walked as if he had a crick in his back.

"I bet I know why he got a sore back," said Larry. "He got it in the closet with all those mops and buckets, bending down with his eye to the keyhole."

Mr. Marvell swore Josh and Larry to secrecy, and they agreed not to reveal a word about the spy in the broom closet.

The very next night the alarm rang again. It was followed by the sound of things falling in the broom closet, then Mr. Marvell's voice roaring, "Come back here, you young devil!"

Josh and Larry fell out of their beds, opened their door, and looked out. Captain Marvell had caught the midnight prowler, a Third Form boy whom they hardly knew. It turned out that he was a well-meaning type who had never been in trouble before but had decided on a little mischief in order to be in the swing of things. It was all part of the midwinter madness at Oakley School. Unfortunately, the authorities took a dim view of the fire-alarm prank and suspended the witless Third Former from school for two weeks. He came back a sadder and a wiser man.

Josh took his guitar to the basement of the sports

building, where he had a locker. It would be safer there than in the broom closet. Already the guitar was looking the worse for wear, and he had not played it once since coming to school. Ali Baba's father had not sent the instrument that you held with your feet, and Scotty had not progressed beyond "Three Blind Mice" on the saxophone. It looked as if their "happening" would not be happening.

As Josh had told Dusty at Christmas time, the winter term was a very busy one. He was working hard on his term paper for Swing Lowe, giving all the reasons he could think of to prove that the *Iliad* and the *Odyssey* were relevant to life today. "We have heroes today," he wrote, "even better than the heroes in the *Illiad* and the *Oddysey*. The Greeks broke down the walls of Troy, but some modern heroes have broken down walls too. An example is Martin Luther King." He wrote several pages about modern heroes breaking down walls. Then he discussed modern explorers. "In the *Illiad* and the *Oddysey* the Greeks were sailing on one sea, the Mediterranean. Now we are sailing in space." He wrote about satellites and astronauts. When he finished his paper he checked the spelling, especially the tricky "Mediterranean," and copied the whole paper neatly. He handed it in on time.

Collecting the papers in class, Swing said, "I do not find one here from you, Brilovich."

"No, sir," said Brillo. "I am going to do something special. May I have some extra time?"

Swing sighed. "I suppose so, but you understand

that lateness counts against you. Mr. Bishop tells me that you have not yet handed in your map of the ancient world. You are your own worst enemy, Brilovich."

"Yes, sir," Brillo said cheerfully, "but I'll really do something special."

"I'll get a low mark," Larry predicted to Josh. "My paper says the *Iliad* and the *Odyssey* are not relevant to life today. Old Swing will blow a gasket."

But when Swing handed back the papers, Larry's mark was 95. A note at the top said, "A neat and well-reasoned paper. I am sorry that you feel as you do, but you are entitled to your opinion."

Josh stared in disbelief at his own paper. It was marked −5. "Cobb," his note read, "this is a very good paper, but you misspelled *Iliad* and *Odyssey* 21 times. There is only one 'l' in *Iliad* and only one 'd' in *Odyssey*. At 5 points each, these misspellings have brought your grade down rather low." Rather low! Josh was fuming with rage. He raised his hand.

"Sir, I only misspelled two words, *Iliad* and *Odyssey,* and you took off 105 points. I don't think that's fair."

"Do not despair, Cobb," Swing told him. "When our head prefect, Alan Crane, was a Fifth Former, he wrote a paper, as I recall, on 'The Uses of the Comma.' It was an inspiring subject, but he spelled 'comma' with only one 'm' and made that mistake fifty times, earning a grade of −150. However, he survived, as you see, and he even ended the year on the honor roll. You may do the same. Meanwhile, if it is any comfort to you, I have chosen your paper and Dunlap's to be read aloud to the class."

Afterward, several boys told Josh they thought his paper was good. Larry walked back to North Hall with him.

"Swing didn't give you a fair grade," he said. "Picking on little things like spelling. No wonder they get him to baby-sit for the Fifth Form. 'Brush your teeth, wash your face, comb your hair!' That's Swing all over. I thought your paper was great. You had a lot of good ideas."

"Yours was good too," Josh said. On this new and friendly note they went together to the mail room. Josh had only the usual weekly letter from his mother, but Larry had something special. He read his letter, grinned, and handed it to Josh.

"Dear Larry," Josh read. "This is just to thank you for the nice time I had at Oakley. Things have been pretty dull since then. We are all counting the days till the spring concert. See you then, I hope. Say hello to your roommate for me. Helen."

Josh felt his heart thumping, but all he said was, "How does she know I'm your roommate?"

"Oh, I told her. She saw you at the game and she saw you at the rehearsal. She told me you bumped into her once on the river. I told her you were on detention for smoking and that was why you weren't dancing. You must have made a hit."

Josh began to see why Larry's opinion of him had changed for the better.

"I want to tell you something," Larry said. "You're

77

the only one I've ever told." He looked around in a guarded way. "I'm going over to town tonight—to the Tuck Shop. Want to come?"

For a moment Josh was silent, staring at his roommate. He did not really want to go to town. Even the idea scared him. Besides, he had just finished working many hours on detention for smoking with Brillo. He was lucky that he had not been put on probation. But it was wonderful to be friends with Larry. It was wonderful to have Larry let him in on a secret, even though he already knew that secret. Best of all, Larry wanted to do something with him, even though that something was illegal.

"I'll think about it," he said.

He thought about it, off and on, all afternoon. Larry was a Big Man on Campus. He was a class officer, an expert skier, a real aristo. He stood high with the faculty too, because he was on the honor roll. And when Helen Crane turned up at Oakley, he walked right off with her. He got along so well, he must know what he was doing.

"But what if we get caught?" Josh asked. They were on their way to their room after dinner, walking along the narrow path that had been shoveled around the Yard by the detention squad. The snow lay waist-deep, and more was falling.

"I never get caught," Larry said calmly. "But don't go if you're chicken."

"I'm not chicken."

"All right, then. We've got two hours to kill. I

have some work to do." On reaching their room, Larry took off his ski jacket, sat down at his desk, and began to work on a chart, putting in the lines neatly and exactly.

Larry could always concentrate. Josh could not. He opened his algebra book and fixed his eyes on one of the problems assigned for the next day. "A river flows downstream at the rate of two miles per hour. Two boats are heading upstream in a four-mile race. Boat X rows at eight miles per hour. Boat Y rows at ten miles per hour. How far apart will the two boats be at the finish of the race? (Give your answer in feet.)"

Without much hope, Josh took a piece of paper and scribbled on it, "X" and "Y." Then he drew a straight river and added some figures and some arrows pointing up and down the river. At the end of half an hour he had covered the paper with figures and arrived at several answers to the problem, but none of them made sense. In some of his solutions the slow boat even won the race, which was obviously impossible.

Josh gave up. He drew a bridge across the river and a road leading to the bridge. He made a small square to the left of the bridge. That was Mr. McGill's house. Josh sat staring at what he had drawn. He was not seeing the piece of white paper. He was seeing in his mind's eye the long stretch of snowy road that led to the bridge across the Mohican River and on into the town. He crumpled his paper and threw it into the wastebasket.

79

Larry completed his own work, folded his paper, and put it away. "Easy," he said. He yawned and stretched. "Might as well knock off some science before we go."

Josh was deep in gloom. "Did you get the one about the boats on the river?" he asked.

"Of course," Larry said. "The slow boat is a mile behind the fast boat at the end of the race. That's 5,280 feet." Quickly he explained the problem. "See, it's simple."

And it was simple. Larry went on explaining problem after problem. They were all simple.

"Gee, thanks," Josh said.

"No problem." Larry went back to his science book.

Filled with gratitude, Josh finished his algebra. What a roommate! Larry was smart all right. He could explain problems better than Mr. McGill.

Suddenly a gong sounded in the corridor. It was the first signal for "lights out."

"Ready?" asked Larry.

Josh nodded. "What do we do now?"

"Wait till everything's quiet."

"What if someone comes in?"

"You worry too much," Larry told him. "Just turn out the light and keep loose." He put on his ski jacket, zipped it up, and got into bed, burrowing down under his blankets.

Josh turned out the light, found his jacket in the dark, put it on, and climbed into his bed. They lay silent, listening to the voices and footsteps of boys

80

who were moving down the corridor toward the wash-room and back again. Doors slammed. The last bell rang for "lights out." All was quiet in North Hall.

Staring into the darkness, Josh lay motionless until his muscles ached, not daring to stir. Then Larry's bed creaked and he knew that the moment had arrived. In the dim light from the lamp outside, Josh saw that Larry was raising the window and stepping over the sill. Quickly, silently, Josh followed. The treacherous snow crunched loudly at every step as they sped from the porch toward the distant river-bank. Josh had never known that snow could make so much noise.

"Not over the bridge," Larry warned in a low voice. "Straight across the ice." Now the darkness covered them, and underfoot the snow seemed to give light for their steps, making escape safer and easier. Larry set the course, expertly avoiding the deep drifts. Lights were on at Gilly's house, but the curtains were closed and all was quiet in that sector. At the edge of the river Larry tested the ice with his heel and ran across, followed by Josh. Following Larry was no problem, Josh thought. He had only to keep loose and not worry.

"From here on, the road is safe," said Larry, scram-bling up the far riverbank. "Don't run, just walk."

Josh could not help asking, "What do we do if we see someone from school?"

"Other guys wouldn't tell," Larry said, "and the faculty don't come to the Tuck Shop at night. They stay home. Mrs. What's-her-name in the Tuck Shop never asks if you have permission to come."

Josh was satisfied. As usual, Larry knew what he was doing.

Around the bend of the road, the lights of the Tuck Shop made a bright patch on the snow, and a moment later its warm interior engulfed them with its sweet chocolaty smell. There was no one in the Tuck Shop except the woman Josh remembered seeing before, the one Larry called Mrs. What's-her-name. She was leaning on the counter, reading a magazine.

They had made it. Josh drew a deep breath of satisfaction and relief as he advanced to the counter. "Mohican Special," he said.

She nodded, picked up a dish and an ice-cream scoop, and began to construct a Mohican Special. Looking at Larry, she said, "Same as usual for you, I suppose. And anything else?"

"I'll take three Crunchees," Larry said, "but nothing else. Chocolate gives me cavities."

Mrs. What's-her-name laughed. "Help yourself." Josh wished she would hurry with the Mohican Special, but she took her time about it, reaching with her scoop into the depths of the counter where the big tubs of ice cream were kept, then dribbling a river of chocolate sauce over the dish in artistic swirls, and topping the whole creation with a mountain of whipped cream shot from a silver spray gun.

While Josh waited, Larry helped himself to three Crunchee bars, left the money on the candy counter, and retired to a back corner where the magazine rack stood. The Tuck Shop stocked magazines not available in the Oakley School library. Happily he hunkered down to read in peace.

Mrs. What's-her-name added a cherry to the Mohican Special and pushed it across the counter to Josh. He paid, picked up a spoon, loaded it to capacity, and opened his mouth wide. At that moment, the front door opened, a blast of cold air struck the back of his neck, and he heard the click-click of a dog's toenails on the tile floor.

A voice behind him was saying, "Good evening, Mrs. Perkins. A quart of vanilla, please."

The dog snuffled at Josh's feet and jumped against him.

"Who's your friend, Winston?" said the voice.

With his cheeks bulging, Josh turned. The abominable Winston looked up at him, smiling and drooling, and Josh was face to face with Winston's master, who said, "Mr. Cobb, I presume."

Josh swallowed. In the silence he heard a faint rustle near the magazine rack. From the corner of his eye he saw the rear door behind the high counter open and close as if someone crouching down had just made a speedy exit.

"Well, Cobb," said Mr. McGill, "I suppose you had permission to come to town tonight."

"No, sir."

Mr. McGill's face fell. "Too bad. However, this is not the time or the place to discuss it. Ah, thank you,

Mrs. Perkins. I believe I have the exact change. Yes. Well. Cobb, please make an appointment to see Mr. Lowe. He makes the decisions about serious offenses by Fifth Form boys. I'm glad I don't have to do it. Meanwhile, you might as well finish that concoction. Waste not, want not. Good evening, Mrs. Perkins."

Josh was left alone with Mrs. Perkins. He laid the spoon on the dish. "I guess I don't want this," he said.

The Mohican Special had cost a lot, but he had lost his appetite.

8

Josh returned to school along the road but decided to enter North Hall by way of the window, on the theory that he already had enough trouble without running into some night watchman who might be on the prowl in the corridors, asking questions and stirring up prefects. The coming interview with Swing Lowe was all Josh could handle.

As he stepped through the window, Larry turned over in bed, asking in a whisper, "What did Gilly say?"

"He said I have to see Swing."

"Oh-oh."

"What do you mean, 'oh-oh'?"

"I mean, tough luck you had to get caught your very first time."

Josh undressed, thinking privately that his first time would be his last. "What does Swing do?" he asked.

"It depends."

On that cheerless note, Josh climbed into his bed. He was in a mess all right, a real mess. He drew his knees up under his chin and pulled the covers over his head.

Strange to say, the sun came up the next morning as if there were no trouble in the world. It shone so brightly that the snow began to melt and to run in rivers along the paths of the yard. There was a definite feeling of spring in the air.

Swing Lowe entered his Fifth Form English class with the stride which meant that the lesson today was one he especially liked. The class had reached the end of the *Odyssey* in their reading. Swing reminded them that Ulysses had now come home. With his great bow and with the help of his son, he had destroyed the unwelcome guests who had troubled his house and his wife during his long absence.

"But did he settle down and grow old sitting by the fire?" asked Swing, as if challenging the class to combat. His fire met no answering fire from Josh, who sat slumped in his desk chair, mulling over his own personal problems; but the rest of the Fifth Form English class answered as one boy, "No!"

"Brilovich, tell us what he did."

"I don't know, sir," Brillo answered. "I haven't got that far."

Mr. Lowe looked annoyed. "Haven't got that far? May I remind you, Brilovich, that we are about to begin studying Shakespeare's *Julius Caesar*? Kindly catch up at your earliest convenience. Even Ulysses took only ten years to come to the end of his journeys."

"I read very slowly and carefully, sir," Brillo said.

"I doubt it," Swing told him. "And by the way, Brilovich, don't forget that you still owe me a paper on the relevance of the *Iliad* and the *Odyssey* to our modern life."

"No, sir, I haven't forgotten."

Mr. Lowe sighed. Once again his gaze roved over the class. "What did Ulysses do at the end of the story?" A dozen hands waved. "What did he do, Mahmud?"

"He started off on his travels again."

"Right," said Swing, with great satisfaction. "Ulysses kept on going to the very end." He picked up a book from his desk and found the page he wanted. "The great Ulysses had some friends who felt the way he did, and this is what he said to them:

"I cannot rest from travel: I will drink
    Life to the lees: all times I have enjoyed
    Greatly, have suffered greatly, both with those
    That loved me, and alone—"

For the first time, Josh perked up. "I have enjoyed greatly, have suffered greatly . . ." Old Ulysses was certainly pretty relevant.

Swing stopped and searched the faces of the class. "Ever feel like that yourself?"

Howie Howland raised his hand. "Sir, what's 'lees'?"

"The lees are the dregs, Howland, the bitter part at the bottom of the cup, when you have drunk the sweet part. Ulysses means that you have to take the bitter with the sweet if you really want to live a full life."

Swing read on.

> ". . . My mariners,
> Souls that have toiled and wrought, and thought
> with me—
> That ever with a frolic welcome took
> The thunder and the sunshine . . ."

Swing interrupted himself. "There it is again, you see—the same idea. A real hero takes things the way they come, the good luck and the bad."

Josh had a queer feeling up and down his spine. Swing Lowe seemed to be talking especially to him, as if he already knew what had happened last night. Or was it Ulysses talking? And if so, what would he say next?

Swing continued, getting more and more excited, pacing up and down as he read:

> ". . . Come, my friends,
> 'Tis not too late to seek a newer world.
> Push off, and sitting well in order smite
> The sounding furrows; for my purpose holds
> To sail beyond the sunset, and the baths
> Of all the western stars, until I die."

Here Swing broke off again. The class sat trans-
fixed, staring back at him. "If any of you go out for
crew in the spring, remember those lines," he commanded. He paused. "How many of you are planning
to go out for crew?"

Under the spell cast by Swing's enthusiasm, every
boy except Brillo raised his hand.

"Now, see how the poem ends—" Swing closed the
book and recited the rest by heart:

> ". . . that which we are, we are;
> One equal temper of heroic hearts,
> Made weak by time and fate, but strong in will
> To strive, to seek, to find, and not to yield."

As he finished the last line, someone at the back of
the room began to clap, and the whole class burst
into applause. Swing looked confused. His face turned
red. "Glad you liked it," he said. "It's by Tennyson,
if you want to look it up. That's all for today."

With a thump, Josh came back from ancient times
to modern days. He must make that appointment to
see Mr. Lowe. As the rest of the class gathered up
books and drifted away, he lingered behind.

"Sir, could I see you about something?"

Swing was in a glow of good humor over the success
of his favorite poem. "Certainly, Cobb," he said.
"What about?"

"Gilly . . . Mr. McGill told me to. I went to town
last night without permission."

Swing's face changed. He looked tired. "Very well,
Cobb. Come at four."

It did not take long for the news to spread through the Fifth Form. Cobb had been caught in town without permission and had to see Swing Lowe. No one seemed to know what the consequences would be. It was the first time this year that such a thing had happened. Certainly, other boys had gone to town without permission, but no one else had been caught. Larry had gone plenty of times and had not been caught.

"Why me?" Josh wondered. He also wondered whether Larry would turn himself in. Josh had turned himself in for smoking in the attic with Brillo. He pictured Larry going with him to Swing's office and saying, "We went to town together." He even imagined Larry taking most of the blame, saying, "I've been going to town without permission all winter. Cobb would never have gone if I hadn't suggested it."

But the day passed without a word from Larry that he had any such intention. He seemed to be avoiding Josh. When Josh went back to their room to wait for the mail, a dozen boys came in to offer their sympathy, but Larry himself did not appear. At lunch Larry found a place at the far end of the table.

Afterward, Brillo met Josh in the Yard and they splashed through puddles together on their way to the science lab, where Brillo was building a model space capsule. "When you go to see Swing, put on a clean shirt," he advised. "He likes that. You know—'Wash your face, brush your teeth, comb your hair,' and all that stuff."

Josh had never felt so lonely and scared. He told T.B. Bishop that he would be absent from hockey practice, and at four o'clock he presented himself at the door of Mr. Lowe's office. He had little hope that Brillo's advice would be of any help, but he was wearing his Oakley blazer and he had polished his shoes. He knocked on the door and went in.

Mr. Lowe was working at his desk, but he stood up when Josh entered, and said, "Well, Cobb, if we're going to have a talk, we had better make ourselves comfortable. Let's have some tea."

He led the way to his apartment, which connected with the office. Josh had heard about Swing's apartment from Brillo, who had been there in the fall to ask to be excused from football. Other boys had described it after being invited because Swing thought they were homesick. Now Josh saw this pleasantly mysterious place for the first time. Its windows looked out on the river. In a fireplace, logs and kindling were ready to be lit, and two chairs were drawn up at a small table. An electric kettle was beginning to steam, and a plate of cookies completed a picture that looked not threatening but friendly and inviting.

Swing said, "Sit down, Cobb, and relax." He lit the fire and made the tea with an expert hand, giving Josh a chance to talk without an eyeball-to-eyeball confrontation. "Tell me what happened last night," he said, and went on fussing with the kettle, the teapot, and a canister of tea.

"Well," said Josh, "I thought I'd go over to town

93

for a Mohican Special." He hesitated. He had not planned what to say and it was hard to tell his story without mentioning Larry. At last he went on. "So I went out through the window and crossed the river on the ice. I was in the Tuck Shop when Mr. McGill came in. I guess that's about it."

Swing looked at him sharply. "Is that all?"

Josh thought a minute. He knew he should tell the truth, but he could not tell the whole truth. He remembered Dusty's words—"Don't be a stoolie."

"That's all I did," he said.

"All right. I'm not going to cross-examine you. Have some tea." Swing handed him a steaming cup and put the cookies on Josh's side of the table. "Help yourself," he said. "And while you eat, I'll tell you what I've been thinking. I've looked over your record for the year so far, and it's quite good. The only problem is that you've spent too much time on detention. You've never done anything seriously wrong, but there it is on your record—detention for this, detention for that, again and again. If there is anything to be learned by raking leaves and shoveling snow, you must have learned it. Do you agree?"

Josh swallowed a mouthful of cookie and mumbled, "Yes, sir."

"But now," Swing went on, "you have done something a little more serious. Mind you, it would probably be all right if you were at home. And at some other schools there might be no such rule. Maybe we should not have this rule at Oakley. Maybe some day we will not have it. But now we do have it. You follow me?"

Josh nodded.

"Some boys," Swing said, "do much worse things, as you well know. That is a dismal subject which we need not go into, but I will tell you that in the upper forms boys are sometimes suspended, or even expelled."

At the word "expelled," Josh's stomach contracted.

"However," Swing continued, "we do not expel Fifth Form students."

Josh's stomach returned to normal.

"Instead," Swing told him, "we assume that a boy needs some extra help in adjusting to his first year away at school. If he keeps on getting into trouble, even mild trouble, we try to find out why. There could be many reasons. Have some more tea."

Josh held out his cup and Swing filled it.

"Many reasons," he repeated. "For one thing, it takes a while to learn the rules. And now and then a boy may break rules just for fun. There's a certain amount of devil in the best of us. There probably should be."

Filling his own cup again, Swing stood up and leaned against the mantel. He looked straight down at Josh and added thoughtfully, "Another reason for getting into trouble is that a boy often feels unsure of himself. Let's say your body has come to school but the rest of you hasn't yet arrived."

Seeing that Josh looked puzzled, Swing explained.

"Until September, you lived at home. It was comfortable, and you knew everybody. Your mother took care of you. Then all at once you found yourself at Oakley. Everything and everybody is new and strange. It is not too comfortable, and there is no one to take care of you. You aren't really homesick, like some boys, but part of you is still at home, needing someone to tell you what to do and to take care of you. So you look around to find someone who seems smarter and better than you are, and you follow his lead. He may not be a good person to copy—a lot of trouble starts that way. One of these days, the missing half of you will come trotting along and catch up with you. Then you'll feel like a whole person, and you'll know who you are. Meanwhile, be yourself, even if you don't yet feel sure of yourself at Oakley. If you're not yourself, you're nobody. 'That which we are, we are,' Cobb."

"Sir?"

"Ulysses," Mr. Lowe reminded him.

Feeling full and comfortable, Josh said, "O.K., sir."

"Now," said Swing, "I know you can make a good record at Oakley. For that reason, I want you to learn to think twice before you get into the habit of breaking a lot of rules. So, here's your penalty for last night. Write to your mother and tell her what you did."

Josh stared up at Swing Lowe. "Write to my mother?"

"Yes. You do write to her, don't you?"

"Not too often," Josh admitted.

"How often does she write to you?"

"Every week." It was slowly dawning on Josh that he would not enjoy writing this letter. "Couldn't I be on probation or something, instead?" he inquired anxiously.

"Definitely not," Swing said, without sympathy. "I know you won't enjoy telling your mother. And don't ask me how to put it. Just put it. One other thing— you'll have to be on detention for a while or it wouldn't seem fair to a lot of other boys who would say, 'Swing let Cobb off too easy.'"

He wandered over to the window and looked out on the river. "Ice is breaking up," he said cheerfully. "The crews will be out on the river before long. The detention squad will be working in the boathouse for a week or so. Hope you'll enjoy it. . . . I mean that."

Josh took this as an invitation to depart, and did so. He spent the rest of the afternoon composing the letter to his mother. No matter how he put it, it looked bad. At last he decided on the sandwich method—first some good news, then the bad news, then some more good news.

"Dear Mother, School is fine. I really like my blazer that you gave me for Christmas. I will wear it when Fairfield, that's a girls' school, comes here for the glee club concert.

"I am sorry I have not written home for quite a while, but thanks a lot for your letters. I enjoyed reading them. I guess you will not enjoy this letter but Mr. Lowe says I have to tell you that I am in

97

some trouble. It is not too bad but it is not too good. I went over to town last night without permission. They have a rule here about that, so it was a dumb thing to do and I will not do it again, don't worry.

"I am still playing goalie and we have won most of our games. I think I will go out for crew as soon as the ice melts. Well, thanks again for everything. I'm really sorry about the bad news. Love, Josh."

He was sealing the envelope when Larry came in, unzipping his ski jacket. "Snow's about gone on the slopes," he announced. "That does it for this season."

Josh was silent.

"What's the matter?" Larry asked. "Feel sick, or something?"

"No," Josh answered briefly. "Swing made me write to my mother."

"Oh. Sorry about that. No, I mean I'm *really* sorry. And I'm never going to town illegally again. Actually, I guess I ought to turn myself in. I know you did, about smoking, I mean. But actually, I mean, I wasn't on too good terms with my family when I was home at Christmas. When I had all those cavities filled, I told the dentist about the Tuck Shop. I shouldn't have told, because he was a real stoolie. He told my father and mother and they hit the ceiling. We're always having arguments. I'm not about to go through all that again." Larry turned his back on Josh, peering into the small mirror over his dresser, combing his hair and frowning as if dissatisfied with what he saw. It came to Josh that his roommate, Larry Dun-

98

lap, class officer, Big Man on Campus, felt unsure of himself, only half a person. The other half of Larry was still at home "having arguments" with his parents. That savvy, that famous savvy, was a lot of bluff. All at once, Josh felt better, as if the missing half of himself had just arrived at Oakley School. He felt like a complete person.

"Come on," he said. "Let's go to dinner." For the first time since they had become roommates, he led the way, and Larry followed.

9

The end of February came and went with a rush. There were times at Oakley when a minute could seem like an hour, but when Josh looked back on the winter term it was like one of the experimental films that some of the upper-class students were making in the film laboratory. Flash, change the scene, flash, change the scene, and the whole thing was over. Afterward, you were never quite sure whether there was a plot or just a constant change of scene.

Josh's mother telephoned in answer to his letter

about the trip to town. He could tell that she was disappointed in him, but she did not say so. Only at the end she said, "Good luck in the spring term, Josh. I'm sure it will be the best one." He knew she meant that it was up to him.

Meanwhile, the winter term at Oakley died in a final fit of madness. There were pillow fights almost every night, until a pillow sailed out a window and landed on the head of a master who happened to be passing below. An epidemic of small insurrections broke out. Just before exams, some Fourth Formers in the North Hall conceived the idea that two of the First Form room inspectors were hounding them. One evening, when the First Form had gone to a dance at Fairfield, a small group of Fourth Form rebels entered the room shared by the two inspectors. They moved the furniture, lock, stock, and barrel, into the shower room—beds, desks, chairs, dressers, and all. When the unlucky inspectors returned from the dance and discovered their plight, they thundered up and down the corridors, howling for revenge; but since there was no specific rule against moving furniture into shower rooms, the rebels got off scot-free. Finally, while the ice was still floating, two boys hacked a great chunk from the edge of the river, borrowed two canoe paddles from the boathouse, and made their way precariously for half a mile downstream before grounding their ice floe at a bend in the river.

Swing Lowe now called for crew practice. At Oakley, baseball headed the list of spring sports, and the tennis courts were always full; but crew attracted enough boys for crews of several weights and different degees of experience. For all of them, Swing set up a schedule of workouts on the rowing machines in the attic of North Hall. Josh had paddled a canoe in his second year at camp, but he had never handled an oar. He reported in the attic with the beginners.

They sat on the floor around Swing Lowe while he introduced them to rowing terms and explained the theory of the sport. "The seats in these rowing machines slide back and forth like the seats in a real boat. You will lace your feet into the leather straps on these wooden struts. They are called stretchers and they are the same as the ones in the boats. When you grasp the wooden handle, it will feel as heavy as a real oar, and you can learn the basic stroke here. But some things you can only learn on the river. For instance, you'll learn on the river how it feels to 'catch a crab.' That is, when your oar is caught in the water and the handle hits you."

The familiar gleam came into Swing's eye. "For beginners the beat in rowing ranges from something like thirty to thirty-eight strokes per minute. The varsity take it up to forty or even forty-two. If any of you saw *Ben Hur,* you can think of it as cruising speed, battle speed, attack speed, and ramming speed." He let this sink in. Then he continued, "You'll hear jokes about crew. They'll tell you that rowing is like beating your head against a brick wall because it feels so good when you stop. They'll tell you that it is the only sport where you sit down and go backward. Another old joke says that no one can teach a rowing man to think, because if he could think, he wouldn't row. Pay no attention. You will never know such team spirit as you have on a crew. You will never feel so fit. Blisters don't count, of course. And to win a race is—well, you probably know it makes you feel so fine that you throw the coxswain into the river." Swing, on fire with enthusiasm, broke off and consulted a list of lightweight boys.

Josh had never heard of throwing the coxswain into the river. It seemed to him like a funny way to thank someone who had helped to win a race, but he made a mental note, just in case he should ever be lucky enough to row on a winning crew.

He was one of the first to step into the rowing machine for the initial workout. After fifteen minutes of practice in pulling on the weighted and tightened wooden handle, he had learned how to "feather his oar" so that the blade would be parallel above the water on the forward swing and upright as he dug into the water for the backward swing. He also found out about blisters.

"You can't judge rowing by a workout with a rowing machine," Swing told them cheerfully. "You can get the feel of an oar by pulling on a handle in a machine. But wait till you pull a real oar on the open river. 'There is nothing, absolutely nothing, like messing about in boats.' "

Those who had read *The Wind in the Willows* grinned reminiscently.

"Next group," said Swing. The workout continued.

In the last class before exams, Swing reviewed the *Iliad* and the *Odyssey*. "We will now be leaving these great epics," he said, "but I trust that you will never forget them." Then he glared at Brillo. "Well, Mr. Brilovich, I have not yet received your paper on the relevance of Homer to modern life. Do you intend to turn it in today?"

"No, sir," said Brillo. "I haven't written a paper."

"You are very foolish, Brilovich," said Swing. "There is really no excuse for your failing the course, but that is what is about to happen. Can you explain why you have made no effort to do this assignment?"

"I have made an effort, sir," Brillo said, not at all downcast under Swing's withering scorn. "I have learned all of Tennyson's *Ulysses*."

After a moment of stunned silence, Mr. Lowe asked, "By heart, Brilovich? All of it?"

"Yes, sir," Brillo said. "I wanted to because it's really great. I like it a lot. And I think it is relevant just when the rowing season is starting."

Swing Lowe was obviously thrown off balance. "Very well, Brilovich," he said cautiously. "Let us hear you recite *Ulysses*. If you can do it, you pass the course."

Brillo came to the front of the class. He folded his arms across his chest, searched the ceiling for inspiration, and began,

"It little profits that an idle king . . ."

Brillo seemed to go into a trance. Not for a moment did he hesitate. On and on he went, line after line, making the class see again the great battles "on the ringing plains of windy Troy" and the perilous voyages over "the dim sea."

Swing Lowe and the Fifth Form English class sat motionless, their eyes fixed on Brillo as he went on, never faltering. At last he took a deep breath and swung into the final passage:

". . . Come, my friends,
    'Tis not too late to seek a newer world.
    Push off, and sitting well in order smite
    The sounding furrows; for my purpose holds
    To sail beyond the sunset, and the baths
    Of all the western stars, until I die.
    It may be that the gulfs will wash us down:
    It may be we shall touch the Happy Isles,
    And see that great Achilles, whom we knew . . ."

In his mind's eye, Josh saw the shield of Achilles, now on exhibit in the school library. Until this moment it had been Brillo's masterpiece, but now he had outdone himself.

"To strive, to seek, to find, and not to yield."

It was over. Brillo looked at Swing Lowe as if to say, "Well?"

As one man, Swing and the Fifth Form English class stood up, applauding and cheering. Swing took out his handkerchief, wiped his eyes, and blew his nose.

"Brilovich," he said, "you couldn't have pleased me more. Reciting a poem is not writing a paper, but this was a real feat on your part." He looked pleadingly at Brillo. "Are you sure you do not want to row?"

"No, sir, it's not my kind of thing."

Mr. Lowe shook his head. "You're hopeless, Brilovich. You really prefer to plant potatoes this spring and water the cows? I don't know what to do with you. But—I must say again, you couldn't have pleased me more."

Exams came and went. When grades appeared, Brillo and Larry were on the honor roll. Josh was not.

"Your winter term was not outstanding, Cobb," said Mr. McGill. "I believe your mind was occupied with trying to find your place here at school. Let us hope that you were only taking a step back in order to make a leap forward. The spring term lies ahead."

After exams, class elections for the spring term were held. Howie Howland became president and G.G. Graham was elected secretary. Larry Dunlap was re-elected treasurer, the only aristo still holding office. When it came to collecting dues and adding up figures, probably no one had such a clear head as Larry. The whole class agreed about that. Josh was no longer as impressed by Larry as he once had been, but he was still proud to be the roommate of the class treasurer.

During the first week in March it rained day and night. The great snowbanks melted fast and the river overflowed. In spite of Mr. McGill's best efforts, the cellar of his house near the bridge was filling with water. He set a problem for the Fifth Form class in mathematics. "Water is flooding into a cellar at 20 gallons per hour. It is being pumped out at the rate of 15 gallons per hour. If the cellar is 20 feet long, 20 feet wide, and 8 feet deep, how many hours will it be until the cellar is full of water?" Josh could not find the answer to the theoretical problem. He was not surprised to hear that Mr. and Mrs. McGill could not find the answer to the real-life problem and were moving off the riverbank to rented rooms in town until the river subsided.

State police and flood-control trucks appeared. The water rose to the level of the bridge and spread out in a lake across half the Lower Field. At last the rain stopped.

Mr. St. Clair made a special announcement in assembly. "We can be very thankful that our school buildings are safe, but you all know that we still have a very serious situation. Emergency conditions will continue until the heavy snows are gone from the hills upstream. The police and flood patrols have enough to do evacuating people from houses up and down the river. We don't want to give them any more trouble. For that reason, and for your own safety, no one here is to go into or near the water. I assume that you have too much sense to do that anyway, but I want to make it crystal clear. We expect the river to subside within the next day or two, but in the meantime any boy who has equipment in the basement of the sports building should remove it."

Josh thought of his guitar. He planned to retrieve it from the sports building as soon as possible, but at the end of assembly Mr. Marvell came into the auditorium with news that changed everybody's plans. Because of the flood, the electric power plant was shut off in all the buildings. The basement of North Hall was beginning to fill with water and upper-class volunteers were wanted to man the hand pumps. Also, the dishwashing machine was not operating, and Fifth Form volunteers were needed for KP duty. Many hands were offered and Josh was among those chosen for kitchen duty. The feeling of emergency put everyone in high spirits. Within the hour, mountains of breakfast dishes had been washed by hand and stacked away.

Josh then put on his slicker and rubber boots. He crossed the Yard, splashed along the edge of the muddy field, and headed toward the sports building. No one else was in sight. Even the police and flood-patrol trucks had gone. Between him and the sports building lay only the wide desolation of the spreading water. The road to town had disappeared and rose above the water only at the bridge. Upstream from the bridge, Mr. McGill's little house stood entirely surrounded by water, which had now reached the first floor. The great oak leaned out, unshaken by the swollen river, but smaller trees along the banks were half submerged.

Suddenly Josh saw in the distant water, near Gilly's deserted house, a small cream-colored object. He stopped and looked again. It was something alive, struggling vainly upstream in the swirling eddies around the sunken abutment of the bridge. It was Winston.

"Dumb dog," Josh said aloud. "Now what am I supposed to do?" He splashed his way to the edge of the flood and called, "Hi, Winston. Come here! Here, you dumb dog." But he knew it was no use. At such a distance the noise of the water rushing at the bridge would drown out the sound of his voice. There was no time to go back to school for help. Even from where Josh stood, he could see snags and whirlpools, any one of which could be the instant death of a small dog.

Gingerly he stepped into the water and started across the Lower Field toward the river, alternately whistling and shouting, "Winston, hey, Winston! Look here! Swim this way!" And suddenly Josh saw the dog's head turning in his direction. The shaggy paws were gamely paddling toward him. Every stroke he swam would carry Winston into shallower, safer water, away from the dangerous currents around the bridge. Josh continued to shout, "Come on, Winston. Attaboy, Winston. Swim! I'm coming."

Now it was harder to wade. The water was almost at the top of his boots and the mud was sucking at them from below. With difficulty, he worked his boots off his feet and waded on, holding his boots above the water.

"Here I come, boy! Good old Winston! Keep swimming!" he called. The dog's eyes were on Josh and he was coming close now, swimming strongly.

"Come on. I'll carry you," Josh said.

He leaned forward to catch Winston and dropped his boots. They floated away. At that moment Winston turned and headed back toward the bridge.

"Stop, you crazy dog!" Josh shouted. He waded on, calling and coaxing, but Winston swam steadily forward, only pausing long enough to look back over his shoulder from time to time, in his usual stupid way.

"I ought to let you drown," Josh muttered, but kept on, getting nearer and nearer to the river. He tried to keep his course upstream, but the surge of the water was very strong now, pulling him inexorably toward the deadly bridge. "Stop, Winston!" Josh cried. "Stop, why don't you?" The water was above his knees. All around him he heard the warning of whispers and sighs that grew in volume as the force of the water drove him closer to the bridge. He had to look down to save himself from debris that floated past, threatening to knock him off his feet with every step he took.

When he looked up again, he saw Winston pinned against the stone abutment of the bridge, caught in a mass of broken branches. All at once Josh knew what to do. Step by careful step he made his way toward the higher ground of the flooded roadway that

crossed the bridge. The water must be more shallow there, so that he could keep his footing and climb up on the bridge where he would be safe above the water and perhaps be able to catch Winston by reaching down.

It was a good plan. His feet felt the incline that banked the road. Then came the security of the asphalt road surface. As he had thought, the water was not so deep here, and the going was good. He reached the bridge, and looked down into the angry water. Below him Winston lay panting, trapped against the abutment. Josh lowered himself until he lay prone and reached down as far as he could. He felt Winston's collar between his fingers. Grasping the collar, he gave a long, strong pull. Winston struggled upward, his nails scrabbling against the bridge, and a moment later Josh had him safe in his arms.

Winston shook himself, spattering muddy water in Josh's face and then licking it clean. "I ought to throw you back in the water," Josh said. "What am I going to do with you? I guess I'd better try to find Gilly in town, if we can get there."

He was still debating the problem when he heard a swishing sound and the honk of a horn. A car was coming slowly along the flooded road from the town. The water came up to the hubcaps and was churned out from the turning wheels like the great yellow wings of some heavenly chariot. Mr. McGill was driving. He pulled to a halt on the bridge and poked his head out of the window. Winston began to bark joyfully.

"What exactly is going on here?" Mr. McGill wanted to know.

"I was going to town, sir," Josh began.

Mr. McGill interrupted him. "You must be out of your mind. You have no more sense than Winston. You're a pair." He pushed open the car door. "Get into this car at once and I'll drive you back to school. Winston, get in here."

Still holding Winston firmly in his arms, Josh tumbled into the car. As they moved slowly along the flooded road to the school, Mr. McGill said, "Now, Cobb, what were you doing on the bridge? Trying to drown Winston? Or going into town for another Mohican Special?"

"No, sir," Josh said. "I was going over to the sports building to get my guitar and I saw Winston in the water. First I tried to get him to come to me, because he always does. But he wouldn't, so I had to go get him."

Mr. McGill's voice changed. "I suppose he had paddled all the way from town to the bridge to see how things were at our house. He's really a very stupid dog. I see you've managed to lose your boots in the process of catching him."

"I couldn't help that," Josh said defensively. "If you'll let me out now, sir, I'll go and get my guitar from the sports building."

"I know you couldn't help losing your boots," said

Mr. McGill. "I didn't mean that. Cobb, I want to thank you for going after Winston. He has really caused you a lot of trouble one way or another. As for your guitar, I'm afraid it's too late to try to save it. Mr. St. Clair has just called me to say that the basement of the sports building is under water."

10

Josh changed his muddy clothes for dry ones and went to lunch in good spirits. Electric power had been restored and the volunteer pumpers, who had worked like Trojans, got the welcome due to heroes when they arrived in the dining hall. Only Mr. McGill was still absent, directing operations in the basement of the sports building, and nothing was said at Josh's table concerning his adventure with Winston.

At the end of lunch, Mr. St. Clair rose and tapped on a glass for silence. Instead of the usual "Dismissed," he said, "I want to congratulate the school on an excellent response to the emergency this morning. Not only our volunteer pumpers but many others did a good job in keeping things under control. I must add that you will be hearing rumors about an incident at the bridge, so I will give you the facts. This morning Joshua Cobb saw Mr. McGill's dog Winston in danger of drowning. He went into the water at some risk to himself and saved the dog's life."

Josh's heart began to beat fast. He was to be congratulated with the heroes!

"However," Mr. St. Clair continued, "you all remember, I am sure, that going into the water is strictly forbidden until further notice. That rule is still in force."

Josh's heart skipped a beat. Was he not a hero after all? Was he really being singled out for a reprimand here and now, before the whole school?

"The rule is still in force," Mr. St. Clair repeated. "But under extraordinary circumstances a rule should be broken. This was one of those times. Good man, Cobb. Like Joshua of old, you have found a way across the river when it was in flood."

Josh heard the whole school clapping and saw a sea of friendly faces turned his way. With his heart pounding, he took a drink of water, choked on it, and grinned feebly. What a day! And all because of "that dumb dog" Winston!

Within a few days the water had subsided, and the Mohican once more flowed placidly between its banks

117

as if it had forgotten the wild raging of the flood. The pale blue sky of spring arched overhead, and the river willows were misted with green.

Long before the Lower Field was dry enough for baseball practice, the men of the flood patrol came to remove from the basement of the sports building whatever was still fit for use. Josh's guitar was a total loss. It had come apart at every seam, and the work crew tossed it into the mud with other flotsam and jetsam. Then a small bulldozer chugged along the road from town and down a ramp into the basement. A crowd of boys gathered to watch the removal of tons of mud deposited there. Presently, the bulldozer chugged back up the ramp and dumped a load of mud into a waiting truck. Josh spotted a tangle of wires and a battered metal hoop.

"There goes my guitar," he said glumly.

But the same day Ali Baba received in the mail a long package, heavily padded, and covered with writing in foreign languages. He brought it immediately to Josh, saying, "Forget the guitar. Here is my sitar. I will teach you to hold it on your foot and we will have our happening."

The unwrapping of the sitar led to the shedding of many shoes and socks, as boys who had come for mail crowded into Josh's room and begged for an experimental plink. But Ali Baba said he could not have a large assortment of strange feet holding his sitar. Only Josh could learn to play if he wanted to.

Before long, the dark pines on the hillsides disappeared behind the bright green of leafing maples, and at last even the ancient oak by Mr. McGill's house came into bud. The rule against going on or into the river was no longer in force, though the water was icy and anyone brave enough to plunge in came out gasping.

One warm day Josh and Brillo saw the McGills on the river in an ancient double shell, an incredibly skinny boat that looked like a mere straw on the water. Gilly was doing most of the work, and Mrs. Gilly was keeping perfect time with lighter oars.

"Gently down the stream," said Brillo. "Gilly's adding a room to his house and he's doing all the work himself. I bet they're going to have a baby. Maybe I can get permission to help Gilly build the new room, instead of milking cows and spreading manure this spring."

Brillo got permission to substitute building for spring sports. Every afternoon, on his way to the boathouse, Josh saw him with Mr. McGill, sawing boards and pounding nails. They looked very happy. So did Mrs. McGill.

Josh could not stop to talk to Brillo these days. As a member of the detention squad, he was helping to repair the dock and the launching raft and to clean and paint the boathouse, where the oars and the long slender shells were stored on racks. Already the varsity crew was on the river every day. Most of them were First Formers. The detention squad would pause, paintbrush in hand, to watch them, eight tall oarsmen and one short coxswain, in white shirts and shorts, jogging along the river path to the boathouse. They entered the boathouse, then emerged with the shell, held keel up at shoulder height, and marched in step to the water's edge. Swing Lowe had promised that the beginners would soon have their first chance to row on the river, so Josh watched every move of the varsity crew. To launch a shell—up, over, and into the water—was no easy matter. It required good timing and balance. When the oarsmen had brought their oars and fixed them into the swivels, the small cox stepped carefully into the boat and held it steady. Next, the portside, moving in unison, grasped the gunwale on either side of the boat and stepped in. With one foot on the footboard, each man lowered himself onto a sliding seat and brought the other foot in, securing both feet to the stretcher. Now they grasped the oars and held the shell steady while the starboard oarsmen took their places. It was a delicate maneuver.

They pushed off. For a few moments the shell lay floating in midstream. Then Josh heard the cox's voice—"Get ready." He could see the change in position as the crew waited for the command, "Ready all." The oars were poised, level with the water. "Ready all . . . row." The oars dipped. The shell slid smoothly away, the torsos above it bending and pulling.

"Push off," Josh thought, "and sitting well in order smite the sounding furrows." Ulysses and his men.

Due to Swing Lowe's enthusiasm, many Fifth Formers had signed up for crew. The first time he went out on the river, Josh's boat was manned by Howie Howland, G.G. Graham, Denny Cheswick, Mead Balfour, Van Stevens, Dan Garrett, and Larry Dunlap, besides himself at the oars, with Scotty Scott as coxswain in the number-three boat, popularly called *Chingachgook*. The number-one and number-two boats, being the newest and the best, were reserved for the varsity and junior varsity crews. Since the boats were fragile—their handmade plywood "skins" so thin that a careless or awkward foot could easily crash through and cause an expensive repair—the beginners were to row in one of the older, less valuable shells, *Chingachgook* or *Uncas*.

Scotty was small and light, but even more important for a cox, he was smart and had quick reactions. He was good-humored, but his voice was crisp and he did not mind barking out orders.

Swing Lowe gave them their places. "Dunlap, we'll try you at stroke. Cobb, take number seven. Graham at six. And two more big ones at five and four, in the middle of the boat. That's the 'boiler room,' where we need the most power." He went on assigning a position to each boy, then guided them through their first uneasy launching of a boat. When it was afloat, they carried down the long oars and fixed them in the swivels as they had seen the varsity crew do. Scotty took his seat. "Hands over." They grasped the gunwale, stepped in, and secured their feet to the stretchers. Boys on the dock helped them push off. This was it.

"Take it easy at first," Swing called, "if you don't

want to wear the skin off your hands—and elsewhere."

Grasping his oar, Josh looked along its length to the blade. The oar was surprisingly long and the blade far away. This was not like practice with the stubby handle in the rowing machine. How would he ever control this oar? Hoping for the best, he leaned forward, knees bent, arms straight, eyes fixed on Larry's neck, just as G.G.'s eyes must be fixed on Josh's neck.

Scotty's voice. "Get ready . . . ready all . . . row." Eight backs straightened and pulled. Eight oars caught the water. Jerkily the shell began to move upstream, following a slow and zigzag course. It was true, as Swing had said a month ago, that you could not judge rowing by a workout with a rowing machine. "Stroke, stroke, stroke," called Scotty, as Larry set the beat.

When they passed under the dark hollow of the bridge, Swing stepped from the dock into a small motorboat and followed them, watching every stroke critically. Conscious of his gaze, the crew pulled on past Mr. McGill's dock.

Josh heard a bark and a faint cheer from the dock. Momentarily taking his eyes from Larry's neck, he saw Brillo waving, with Winston at his feet. That moment threw Josh off balance. He lost the rhythm of the stroke and felt his oar digging too deep. The weight of the water wrenched the oar handle from his grasp. The handle hit him in the chest, knocking the wind out of him, then lifting him out of his seat and into the river. When he came to the surface,

122

gasping with the shock of the cold water, he saw all the oars on his side of the boat thrashing wildly, and the boat itself still moving upstream.

"Weigh, 'nuff—easy all," Scotty ordered, and the oars came to rest. The beginners' crew drew breath and looked back in consternation at Josh's head, bobbing behind them.

Then Swing Lowe was grinning down at him from the motorboat and saying, unsympathetically, "No sweat, Cobb. All good oarsmen fall in at least once. You are rather wet and muddy. Swim out and change your clothes. Then come straight to the boathouse for a debriefing."

Josh swam to the dock and pulled himself onto it with a helping hand from Brillo, who said scornfully, "Debriefing. What a sport. Swing won't care if you drown as long as you learn good form first."

Winston jumped up on Josh, scratching his bare legs with sharp toenails and looking into his face with loving eyes. Josh thought it was too cold for conversation. He pushed Winston away and went off to change.

The rest of the crew, under Swing's directions, turned the shell and finished their maiden voyage at the boathouse dock, minus one oarsman, but without further accident. Josh reached the boathouse in time to help with the tricky business of hauling the shell from the water and returning it to the rack. Swing supervised Scotty in the coxswain's duty of wiping down the shell with a chamois, then gathered the whole crew around him for the debriefing. There were a hundred kinds of faulty technique, and Josh seemed to be guilty of all of them; every one of the crew had rowing mistakes to correct. "You looked like a wounded snake going upstream," Swing concluded, "and even worse coming back, but not hopeless. Remember to keep loose. You've got possibilities. See you here after your last class tomorrow."

That was the first of many afternoons on the river. Scotty's voice seemed to be always in their ears, "Stroke, stroke, stroke . . . take it up to thirty-four . . . steady . . . take it up to thirty-six." Cruising speed, battle speed, attack speed, ramming speed. When the beat reached thirty-six, Josh knew what ramming speed must have felt like to Ben Hur. But, rowing behind Larry, he would pull his arms out of his shoulder sockets to keep up the beat set by Larry. Swing's debriefings were always severely critical, but he kept his oarsmen just short of despair, egging them on to do better, sending them away determined to improve. He kept them on a strict diet of meat, vegetables, fruit, and plenty of milk. No candy. Slowly but surely, they did improve.

There came a day when Mr. McGill said at lunch, "The beginners' boats seem to be shaping up." He turned to Josh and added, "Stop by at my house after crew practice, Cobb. You might like to look at my double shell."

Josh was mystified, but he accepted the invitation and after practice went directly from the boathouse to

Gilly's house, jogging along the river path in the late-afternoon sunshine. As Swing had predicted, he felt wonderful after rowing. Winston came bounding to meet him and raced beside him on the last stretch, barking joyfully.

The outside walls of the McGills' new room were finished, and Gilly himself was on the roof, nailing down shingles. At first, Josh did not see Brillo. Then he spotted a tall ladder leaning against the great oak tree. High above the ladder, Brillo straddled a broad limb.

Mr. McGill paused, hammer in hand. "Evening, Cobb," he said, and then, following the direction of Josh's gaze, "Great climber, Brilovich. Always was, since the first time I caught him in the bell tower. Now he's making measurements for a tree house. I've told him he can build one with the leftover lumber. Come on down, Brilovich. The scull is in the garage."

Brillo climbed down the ladder while Mr. McGill went on, "Fact is, seeing you row past every day, Brilovich has been thinking he'd like to get out on the river—not with the crew, but on his own. Never has had a pair of oars in his hands, so I thought you might go together for a starter. Give him the hang of it. If you enjoy it, come any time you like. It will be a way to thank him for his help on the new room and to thank you for helping Winston out of the flood."

Both boys knew enough about the value of a sculling shell to appreciate this generosity. As they launched the slender shell and carefully pushed off, he called, "It tips over easily, so watch your balance."

Managing an oar in each hand was a new experience for Josh, but he learned quickly, and so did Brillo. They learned a lot—how to row without disturbing the smooth run of the boat, how to make an oar catch hold of the water without undue splashing, how to find and maintain a good rhythm. Josh rowed at stroke, with Brillo behind him.

Usually the McGills' shell was ready and waiting for them when Josh met Brillo at the little dock after crew practice, but some days the owners were out on the river themselves when the boys arrived, rowing together so smoothly that it gave Josh an idea. The glee-club concert was not far off. Rowing had been taking so much of his time that he had almost forgotten that event, but now the idea of it came back with a rush.

At the next Job Assembly Mr. St. Clair reminded them, "A week from Saturday will be the date of the glee-club concert with Fairfield. And speaking of dates, if any of you want to ask a girl for a date, you had better write to her at once. The Establishment up there at Fairfield would take a dim view of two hundred telephone calls, so please do not telephone. As for entertainment that weekend, you might like to mention the debate on Saturday afternoon. The debating teams will be putting on a good show, I am sure. Let me see—I believe their subject is: If chivalry has died, it should return."

He was interrupted by laughter and a few groans,

but continued, "If the debate does not appeal, you can get permission to go into town to the Tuck Shop during the afternoon, with or without a date." Unanimous applause and cheers followed this announcement. "In other words," the Saint concluded, "you can do pretty much what you like, as long as you get permission."

Josh approached him immediately after the Assembly. "Sir, can I take a girl out sculling on the river in Mr. McGill's shell, if he says so?"

Mr. St. Clair nodded. "A magnificent plan, Cobb," he said solemnly. "Just make sure she can swim. If sculling doesn't get her, nothing will."

But when they returned to North Hall after Job Assembly, complications set in. As Josh and Larry reached their door, Brillo paused there long enough to announce, "I'm asking Becky Goodall for a date."

Then Larry dropped a bomb. "I'm asking Helen Crane."

"But I'm asking her," Josh said. "I've got it all planned."

"So what?" Larry shrugged. "I've been planning it all along. And you don't even know her, not really."

It was true. Josh hardly knew Helen. But hadn't she written to Larry, "Say hello to your roommate for me"? She knew who he was, anyway.

He sat down at his desk. "I'm going to write to her," he said stubbornly. He drew out an envelope and a piece of paper and began, "Dear Helen, Maybe you don't remember me, but I remember you. I bumped into you skating on the river and I saw you

at the Oakley hockey game and at the glee club rehearsal and at the dance. How are you? Everything
is fine here. I guess you will be coming to Oakley for
the glee club concert. Will you go sculling with me
on the river if you can swim? Please let me know.
Sincerely, Josh Cobb."

When he finished, Larry was sealing an envelope of
his own, and the two letters went out by the noon
mail to Miss Helen Crane at Fairfield School.

That night Josh dreamed that Larry had run away
from school, taking all the class funds with him, and
he, Josh, caught him and made him give back the
money. For the rest of the week, during crew practice
when his eyes were fixed on the back of Larry's neck,
he wanted to wring that neck. Swing detected that
something was wrong and more than once picked
Josh out for unfavorable comment. "Cobb, remember that Dunlap is rowing stroke. Try to keep with
him. You're supposed to be pulling together. And
you're all tensed up. Keep loose."

That was easy to say, but hard to do. It was a relief
to get away from the boathouse and go up the river
path on a sunny afternoon two days before the concert. Josh looked through the window of the McGills'
new room, but no one was there. Work was evidently
over for the day. He looked up into the big oak tree
and saw Brillo lying flat on a platform high in the
branches. Brillo poked his head over the edge of the
platform and waved.

"Come on up," he called. When Josh had climbed

128

up by way of wooden struts nailed to the trunk and hauled himself through a hole in the platform, he found Brillo obviously pleased with himself. "Pretty neat, isn't it?"

"Sure is," Josh said. He meant it. Below them flowed the river, with black tree trunks reflected shivering in its shining mirror. Up and down stream, whichever way he looked, he saw a double image of spring green along the riverbanks. The bridge had a double arch, a real one of iron girders above, and an upside-down, watery one below. Beyond the bridge, the roofs of town were almost hidden among the tree-tops. Josh sat down and took it all in, his legs dangling over the edge of the platform. "Gee, I like it here," he said.

"You ain't seen nothing yet," Brillo told him. "I'm going to put up posts at each corner and have a roof. Maybe some low walls too, so I can sleep here and not fall off. But first I'm going to bring Becky up for a picnic Saturday afternoon. If you've got a date, you can bring her up too."

"I don't think I've got one," Josh said.

But the next day changed things. In his mailbox, that unpromising little pigeonhole that never had anything in it except his mother's weekly letter and an occasional one from Dusty Moore, there was an unfamiliar blue envelope. Tearing it open, he broke through the crowd of boys who were still waiting for mail and carried his letter into his room.

"Dear Josh," he read, "It was nice to hear from

you. When you get this, it will be almost time for the concert and we are certainly getting excited. Thank you for asking me to go sculling with you. I have never done it but it sounds like a lot of fun. I can swim. Well, I'll see you Saturday. Sincerely, Helen Crane. P.S. My brother Alan says you saved a dog's life in the flood. Great!"

Josh was reading this letter for the third time when Larry walked in. Josh almost felt sorry for him. "I heard from Helen Crane," he told Larry. "I've got a date with her to go sculling."

"That's all right," Larry said calmly. "I heard from her too. I'm taking her to the dance."

With a dull thud, Josh came back to earth. Why hadn't he thought of the dance? "Oh," he said. Then he considered the situation and cheered up. "Anyone can take a girl to a dance. If you've seen one, you've seen 'em all. Sculling's a little different. Also, I'm taking her to a picnic in a tree house."

Saturday dawned bright and warm, and the Fairfield buses arrived promptly at noon. Half the boys at Oakley milled about the buses. Some came to find their dates and take them to lunch, the rest came to watch and to envy. Josh saw Larry strolling about with his hands in his pockets, playing it cool, but scanning every face that appeared in the bus doorways.

Suddenly there she was, smiling and jumping down from the bus step with a small suitcase in her hand. She was wearing a yellow skirt and a yellow turtle-

130

neck sweater. She flipped her long hair back over her shoulders and looked around. Josh waved and started forward, but Larry reached her at the same moment.

She looked from one to the other. "Oh," she said. "Hi." She looked at a spot halfway between them and asked, "What do we do now?"

As usual, Larry had all the answers. "I think you're all supposed to go to the guest house and leave your things there. Then, can I have a date for lunch?"

Josh could have kicked himself for not thinking of it. But Larry's savvy was in vain this time. "Oh, thanks," she said, "but I have to have lunch with my brother," and she smiled up at someone behind them.

"Right," said Alan Crane, and took her away.

Neither of them saw much of her until after lunch, but Josh told Brillo he had his date, and Brillo said, "I've got Becky. I'm taking her to the debate. Then we'll meet you at the tree house. Bring some Cokes or something."

The moment lunch was dismissed, Josh dashed across the dining hall and was waiting at the door for Helen Crane when she came out.

"Stay here," he said. "I've got to get something. Wait right here. Don't go away. I'll be right back."

He sped off to the supply store. But there was a crowd around the counter. It took him ten minutes to buy a bag of potato chips, a package of cookies, and two bottles of Coke, and it seemed more like an hour. He ran all the way back to the dining-hall door. She was still there, and Larry Dunlap was there too.

When he saw Josh coming, he laughed and said something. Josh did not hear what he said, but he was sure he knew. "Here comes Corn Cobb."

"All set," Josh panted. He spoke only to Helen, leaving Larry out of it, but Larry asked her with exaggerated politeness, "Mind if I come too?"

Again Helen looked from one to the other. "It's a free country," she said. "Where are we going?"

Josh set off at a fast pace, his arms full of bags and bottles. Helen and Larry followed, across the Yard and along the edge of the lower field. Presently, Larry reached out and took Helen's hand. He held it until they reached Mr. McGill's house, where he let it go, but not before Josh had turned and seen them hand in hand.

Aloud, he only mumbled, "You might as well wait here a minute," but inwardly he thought of words his mother had told him never to say. Leaving Helen and Larry together, he jogged off to the big oak tree. He stuffed the two Coke bottles into his pockets and climbed the struts up the trunk to the platform, depositing his burden there and wishing never to see it again. He had studied leeches in science and knew they were one of the lower forms of life. Now he had seen one and its name was Larry Dunlap. Well, he would be rid of him once he got Helen into Gilly's double shell, where there was only room for two. He picked up the oars from Gilly's front porch.

When he returned, Helen was standing with her hands clasped behind her back and looking down thoughtfully at a circle that she was marking in the dirt with the toe of her shoe. Larry looked as if he thought she was Helen of Troy.

"Come on," Josh said to her gruffly. "I mean, do you want to?"

"Sure," she said in her soft, deep voice, and she gave him a sideways smile. "I really do."

"I'll help you launch the scull," said Larry.

Josh knew what he wanted to do—punch Larry in the nose, take Helen's hand, and make a run for it. But, instead, he turned on his heel and again let them follow. When the scull was launched, Josh knelt to put the oars in the swivels and tighten them there. Then, still kneeling, he commanded Helen, "Get in. You sit in the bow."

He saw Larry offering a hand to help Helen into the scull and glared at him. "I get the message," Larry said, and withdrew to the far end of the dock, where he stood watching with a skeptical air. "Look out," he called. "It tips."

Josh pushed off. "Hold your oars straight out just above the water," he ordered, "until I work her into midstream."

From behind him he heard her voice. "I've been in a rowboat. Just tell me what to do." She sounded humble and Josh's spirits rose.

He began to teach her, as he had taught Brillo. But there was a difference. Brillo was as big as Josh, and as strong. During the winter both of them had grown a lot. They were evenly matched. Helen rowed well

133

for a girl, Josh thought, but she was neither as big nor as strong as he was. Conscious of this fact from the pull of her oars, and knowing that her eyes were fixed on the back of his neck, he felt six feet tall and as strong as Hercules. He gave a mighty pull on his oars and turned his head to see whether Larry was still watching.

A scull floats beautifully level when it is empty. If there is someone in it, there are a number of ways to tip it over. One error is to transfer your weight slightly to one side. Another is to press harder with one foot. Still another way is to bear down more heavily on one oar handle. As Josh turned to see whether Larry was on the dock, he made all three of these errors and the shell tipped over.

Josh plummeted into the icy water, then frantically reversed himself and scrambled to the surface. He looked for Helen. No sign of her. She was still under-water and he must dive for her, no matter how deep the Mohican might be. He took a big breath, jack-knifed, and made a surface dive. As he went down he collided with a blur of bright yellow. He clutched it and came to the surface again. Helen's head was bobbing beside him. She was pushing back her long wet hair and she was laughing.

"You sure you're all right?" he sputtered.

"Of course I'm all right," she said. "I'm a good swimmer. Come on, I'll help you push the boat to shore."

From the dock came a splash, followed by the

sound of a dog's urgent barking. Looking ahead, Josh saw Larry swimming strongly toward them. Winston was on the dock, obviously eager to join the community swim, and Mr. McGill was hurrying from his house. With a few strokes Larry reached the boat.

"Need help?" he asked, and took hold of the gunwale. As the three swimmers brought the shell close to the dock, Mr. McGill leaned down to give Helen a hand and said, "Really, Cobb, was this swim necessary? You and Dunlap had better tie up the shell. You can bail it out later. This young lady needs more dry clothes than she has brought with her, I suspect. I'm driving my wife to the hospital. Then I'll drive your friend back to Fairfield. Someone else can return her in time for the concert."

Mrs. McGill came out with a blanket to wrap around Helen and took her into the house. Josh and Larry were still working on the dock when Gilly put Helen and Mrs. Gilly into his car and drove off. Mrs. Gilly was carrying a little suitcase. Helen waved back to them and got two answering waves from the dock.

"Some girl," said Larry.

"Right," Josh said. "Some girl."

They saw Brillo and Becky coming along the river path, carrying a basket between them.

"Debate's over," Brillo said. "Time for the picnic." Then—"Gee, you look as if you've been in the river."

"We have," Josh said. "I won't be coming to the picnic. You can eat my stuff."

"What's happened?" Brillo wanted to know.

"Nothing," Josh told him. "Except I guess Mrs. McGill has gone to have a baby. Everything's fine." And considering that Helen did not seem to be mad at him, he meant it. Everything was fine.

11

Word of the adventure soon spread. Some said that Josh had saved Helen Crane's life and was going to be given a medal. Others said that Josh had dumped her in the river and that Larry Dunlap had saved her. One girl declared she knew for a fact that Helen had walked all the way back to Fairfield swearing that she would never return to Oakley or speak to Josh and Larry again.

Helen was not among the girls who crowded into the Oakley dining hall for dinner that night. And

Howie Howland, passing plates, said, "I hear you guys were trying to drown Helen Crane and she's never coming back here."

Captain Marvell, seated at the head of the table in Gilly's absence, squelched Howie at once. "Howland, for your information, Dunlap and Cobb both tried to rescue a lady in distress this afternoon. It was not their fault that she happened to be a good swimmer and didn't need to be rescued. Also, if you didn't know, the affirmative side won the debate this afternoon. Remember? 'If chivalry is dead, it should return.' Dunlap and Cobb have just been proving that chivalry is not dead—not at Oakley, anyway. Incidentally, I'm driving to Fairfield to pick up the lady immediately after dinner. She'll be here for the concert."

She was. When the combined glee clubs converged on the stage, Josh saw her right away as the two groups milled about, finding their places.

"You O.K.?" he asked.

"I'm fine," she said. "Don't worry." Her hair seemed to be dry, as far as he could tell. He was glad of that.

Magnificent in his green blazer and feeling like a million dollars, Josh made his way to the risers at the back of the stage, where he would take his place between G.G. Graham and Brillo. Fairfield was massed in front of Oakley, wearing white dresses and blue scarves. The faculty of both schools had come, and there was even a sprinkling of parents, so that the auditorium was filled to the rafters. Josh could see the back of Helen's head below him in the front row.

Now the footlights were on and the auditorium was dark. Swing Lowe raised his hands. The combined glee clubs opened their concert.

> "The fox went out on a chilly night
> And prayed to the moon to give him light;
> He'd many miles to go that night
> Before he'd reach the town-o."

That was a good one. Josh liked it even more than he had when he and G.G. had first sung it together crossing the Yard last fall, long before he had gone out with Larry on a chilly night and got himself into a lot of trouble to "reach the town-o."

Next, Oakley sang "Sometimes I Feel like a Motherless Child," and Swing looked well-pleased when they stretched out the last word in a thoroughly professional manner: "A long way from ho-o-o-me." Last fall, when they had first sung that song, a lot of Fifth Form "brats" would almost cry. Most of them had been like small scurrying animals, trying merely to exist under hard, new conditions. Now the first year was almost over. A few of the new boys had left Oakley, unable or unwilling to adapt to life away from home. But most were here tonight. They were the survivors. They had discovered ways to live and even to enjoy life as individuals in an institution "a long way from home."

Josh was too much involved in following Swing's

139

direction to think these thoughts clearly, but they were there somewhere under the music, and they gave him new and pleasurable feelings.

Now it was time for the Fairfield specialty, that medley of TV commercials which had made such a hit at the rehearsal in February. While Fairfield sang, the Oakley glee club was not to move a muscle; even though Josh could not see Helen, he thought he could hear her voice among the others. The TV commercials brought down the house and spurred Oakley on to outdo themselves with "Joshua Fit the Battle of Jericho."

Josh had always felt self-conscious about this one, tonight more so than ever. The Biblical Joshua had had adventures with a river, and so had Josh, trying to cross it in the flood, rowing on it, falling into it. Maybe nobody else was thinking about him, but to Josh it seemed that this was really his song.

> "Joshua fit the battle of Jericho, Jericho, Jericho;
> Joshua fit the battle of Jericho
> And the walls came tumbling down."

The audience liked it so much that Oakley had to sing another chorus. When the applause died down, the accompanist from Fairfield took her place at the piano and Swing led the girls into "Coming through the Rye." Josh thought it was great, but he was mostly waiting for Helen's solo. First the girls all together,

> "If a body meet a body, coming through the rye,
> If a body kiss a body, need a body cry?

Every lassie has her laddie, nane they say have I,
Yet all the lads they smile on me when coming
  through the rye."

There it was, Helen's voice singing alone, soft and
clear,

"Amang the train there is a swain I dearly love
  mysel',
But what his name or where his hame I dinna
  choose to tell . . ."

Did she like him best, or Larry? So far, she certainly did not "choose to tell." Maybe only time
would tell. Meanwhile, with the rest of the Oakley
glee club, Josh was roaring out, "There Is Nothing
like a Dame." There was no argument about that,
anyway. They all agreed that there was nothing like
a dame.

At the very end of the concert there was a complete
surprise. Some of the Oakley faculty came on stage to
sing a song that they had prepared with well-kept
secrecy. The teachers Josh knew best were among the
dauntless performers. There was T.B. Bishop, who
had coached him in hockey and for whom he had
drawn his enormous map of the ancient world. Now
Mr. Daily was taking his place in the lineup—the
Daily Grind, who had coached Josh in the first wonderful days on the football field. Josh would be getting to know him as a teacher next year when he
started Latin.

The Saint was the central figure of the whole group,
a really great headmaster, Josh thought, remember-

ing how he got everyone to talk and argue in Bible Studies. Joshua and the walls of Jericho! He would never forget that story. He would never forget how the Saint had made the whole school pull together during the flood. At Swing's signal, the music swelled up and out over the auditorium.

"I'm gonna lay down my sword and shield, down
    by the riverside,
Down by the riverside, down by the riverside;
I'm gonna lay down my sword and shield, down
    by the riverside,
Ain't gonna study war no more."

After a year at Oakley, Josh knew the faculty backs as well as he knew their faces. Captain Marvell was singing with all his might. His hair was long enough now to curl down almost to his shirt collar. Who would have thought that the skin-head who presided over the detention squad last fall in the potato field would grow so much hair by spring? Gilly's neck and ears were red. He had arrived at the last minute and could hardly stand still as he sang. Everyone knew why he looked so happy and flustered. Mrs. Gilly was in the hospital in town, and Gilly was the father of a baby, a boy, born that afternoon. Good old Gilly. He had let Josh use his double shell, and he had helped him a lot this year, patiently explaining problems until algebra no longer made Josh lose his appetite. He had got the hang of the thing at last.

Swing was leading. He was really putting out tonight, but then he always did. It was partly because of Swing that Josh liked the glee club so much. He picked out good songs and he made you sing your best. It was because of Swing that Josh had gone out for crew, the greatest sport yet. And Swing had helped him out of a bad spot, getting him straightened out after the illegal evening at the Tuck Shop. Swing had helped Josh find himself and be himself. "That which we are, we are, Cobb." Good old Swing.

With a big gesture of his arms, Swing let the glee clubs know that they must join in, and out in the darkness they heard the audience singing too, taking up the melody one by one until all were singing together and the whole room was filled with it.

> "Ain't gonna study war no more, ain't gonna study
> war no more,
> Ain't gonna study war no more."

It was a great end to a great concert. They all felt it so much that nobody could really talk about how they did feel. Instead, as soon as possible, the glee clubs broke up and began looking for their dates. Josh saw Larry coming up the stage steps and making a beeline for Helen. Fair enough. She was Larry's date for the dance, and since this afternoon, Josh wasn't "gonna study war no more" with Larry. Anyhow, he could always break in and get some dances with her himself. He thought he could remember how to boom, trap, trap fairly well, and now he was even glad he had had to trudge across the old gym floor at home with those dumb girls. It came in handy on a night like tonight. There would also be a lot of times when they turned up the record player full blast and all you had to do was sort of jump around. He thought he could do that all right.

The ever-busy detention squad had made decorations which Brillo had designed for a Glo-Ball that would outshine even the glorious memory of the winter Snow Ball. This time a dozen silver satellites and spacecraft hung as if suspended in mid-air above the dancers. Nobody could see the thin black threads from which the accurate models floated and twirled. One end wall of the recreation room was covered with a huge poster showing a map of the earth, its blue seas and green continents all clearly recognizable, as astronauts would see it when they launched out from Cape Kennedy. On the opposite wall a poster showed a map of the moon, round and white, covered with mountains and craters and great dry seabeds, as it would appear to space voyagers approaching from the earth. The effect was breathtaking.

Brillo, with Becky by his side, was receiving congratulations and looking pleased with himself.

"Brilovich," said T.B. Bishop, "I have not yet received the map of the ancient world that you owe me. But you have made a map of the present world and a map of the world of the future, as it were. Consider yourself in the clear."

Still on probation for smoking, Brillo could not dance but, in his opinion, making a splash with his decorations was the best part of the dance anyway.

144

When Josh arrived to add his own congratulations, Brillo could hardly spare a moment to talk.

"Where did you get the idea for all this?" Josh wanted to know.

"From your paper about the *Iliad* and the *Odyssey*," Brillo said. "Remember? You said that Ulysses just explored the Mediterranean, but modern explorers were sailing in outer space." While Brillo talked he was looking over a pile of records. "We've got to find every record about the moon or night," he told Becky. "It should be easy. You look in that pile and I'll take this one. We'll find plenty."

"Oh, good idea," she said, but Josh thought she did not sound enthusiastic. She kept looking off toward the dance floor and tapping her foot.

Josh went off to find Helen. As he had expected, she was already dancing with Larry, who had never looked more like an aristo. He was holding her lightly and securely, circling slowly with her around the floor, talking and laughing, playing it cool. Josh did not have enough nerve to break in.

He thought about asking Becky to dance. He was sure she wanted to. But Becky was Brillo's date. If Josh asked Becky, Brillo would be left alone.

Finally Brillo changed the record to a dance that Josh had learned to do at home. Boom, trap, trap, boom, trap, trap—an oldie but goodie. It was now or never, Josh decided. He dashed across the floor, collided with Helen and Larry, and asked, "Break in?"

"Sure," Larry said casually, and moved away.

"I keep bumping into you," Josh said. He drew a deep breath, took Helen's hand, and put his arm around her. Then he waited a moment to get the rhythm of the music—boom, trap, trap, boom, trap, trap—and they set off. Josh did not try to talk. He had his work cut out for him without talking. Still, things seemed to be going pretty well. She was following easily.

Carefully, cautiously, Josh steered Helen down the length of the recreation room. But when they reached Brillo's moon, he was stuck. He had never really learned to negotiate a turn on the dance floor. Helen was pinned against the wall and he was helpless to budge her unless he picked her up bodily and heaved her around. Why didn't Larry come and break in, he thought desperately.

Then the wonderful girl came to his rescue. "What's the name of the boy who's playing the records?" she asked. "Let's go over and talk to him. He's all alone."

"Who? Brillo?" Josh said. He turned to look. Brillo was indeed all alone, and Larry was dancing with Becky. That old savvy!

Walking, not dancing, Josh and Helen made for Brillo's corner. "Sorry I'm not much of a dancer," Josh mumbled.

But Helen said, "What do you mean? I thought you were great." She really was some girl!

For the rest of the evening Josh danced with Helen as much as possible, sticking to those dances where the record player was turned up full blast and the dancers jumped around with no turns to negotiate. When anyone else broke in, he retreated to Brillo's corner to keep him company, but Brillo did not seem to be lonely. He never was lonely, Josh guessed, because he kept so busy thinking up new ideas. Becky did not reappear in Brillo's corner. She was dancing every dance.

Josh managed to get the last dance with Helen, and when Larry came to take her to the bus, Josh stayed with them. "Mind if I come too?" he asked. After all, he had learned some things from Larry. So, when the recreation-room lights were turned out on the paper moon, they walked out, all three together, across the Yard, with a real moon shining in the sky above them.

"When are you coming back?" Larry asked.

"Maybe not until June," Helen said. "I'll come then because my brother is graduating, of course." On the step of the bus she turned and smiled down at both of them. "You could write to me," she said. Then the door closed behind her and the bus rolled away into the night.

"I have something to do," Larry said. "See you later." Tonight everyone had late permission until midnight, so Josh went to bed without undue curiosity about where Larry was going or what he was going to do.

Josh fell asleep fully intending to write Helen every day of his life, but the next day, before he could write even the first letter, something happened which took every spare minute. Swing Lowe ordered two boats of beginning oarsmen to report to the boathouse and he started to train them for racing.

The number-four shell, *Uncas*, was already in the water when Josh came through the boathouse door. He saw Swing talking to Larry and heard him say, "Dunlap, you have chocolate on your teeth."

Josh went on about his own business, joining the rest of the crew, who were watching Scotty Scott as he removed the oars from the racks and greased them. None of them could help hearing Swing's continued remarks.

"You have been rowing at stroke, Dunlap. I gave you that responsibility because I thought you could handle it. How did you happen to break training?"

Larry maintained his usual calm. "I just went into town last night on late permission," he said. "I bought a few chocolate bars. Sometimes I get a yen for chocolate."

Without an answer, Swing turned away, and the crew lowered *Chingachgook* from its rack. They carried it down to the dock and put it into the water. Now they would test the results of Swing's careful coaching during the past month. No longer would they be rowing only to improve their form and to beat their own best time by Scotty's stop watch. Today was different.

Before he sent them into the boat, Swing lined them up on the dock and told them what he had already told the crew of the *Uncas*. "You have to be physically strong to race, and you need good technique, but most of all you need the will to win. That's more important than all the technique in the world. There are some men who always seem to win, even though they do everything wrong. So today don't worry about form. And may the best crew win."

The two shells took their positions side by side in midstream. Grasping his oar, Josh fixed his eyes on Larry's neck and waited for Scotty Scott's command. "Get ready . . . Ready all . . ." From the shore came Swing's voice. "Get ready . . . Are you ready? . . . Row!"

In unison the oarsmen dug their blades into the water and both shells began to move upstream. Josh knew that *Uncas* was moving beside them but he did not turn his head to see it. That was Scotty's business. His own world was reduced to the sound of Scotty's voice, "Stroke, stroke, stroke . . ." and the rhythmic beat of the wooden knobs on the rudder lines in Scotty's hands as he steered them upchannel, the sight of Larry's back and his dipping oar, the feel of his own legs thrusting against the stretchers, his own arms pulling, his own back bending.

Now Scotty was increasing the beat. "Take it up to thirty-six." Was *Uncas* pulling ahead? Or was Scotty trying for a sprint? The crew of *Chingachgook* responded to the quickened pace. A shadow covered them and was gone. They had passed under the bridge. Josh heard the putt-putt of a motorboat; Swing was following them. Keeping well out of their way, he outdistanced them. He would be waiting at the finish line a mile up the river.

Once again Scotty was increasing the beat. "Take it up to thirty-eight." Suddenly, without turning his head, Josh saw *Uncas*. It was falling behind, its crew unable to keep up the fast pace set by *Chingachgook*.

"Half mile," Scotty said. "Steady." They were half a length ahead of *Uncas*. Now a full length ahead. There was open water between the two boats, widening every minute, and they were on the last stretch. This, then, was how it felt to win a race!

And all at once Josh saw Larry swaying from side to side, his oar trailing in the water. Larry was holding the gunwale and leaning out. He was being sick into the Mohican River.

12

"Which proves," said Swing, "that the slow boat does sometimes win the race, if its crew pulls together, has the will to win, and never gives up." He had gathered the two crews around him on the dock for the debriefing after the race. "*Uncas,* you did well today. Keep it up. *Chingachgook* had a little trouble. Dunlap tells me he broke training and ate quite a lot of chocolate. Result—under stress, he got sick, and the whole boat fell apart. At this point we'll try a change. Graham, move to stroke tomorrow, and Dunlap, take six. Dismissed."

"You should have got it," Brillo said, when Josh told him the news.

"It wouldn't have worked," Josh said. "It's bad to make a switch from port to starboard. Stroke, six, four, and two can switch, because they all row on the port side. I row seven. I could switch with five, three, or bow. But if I moved from seven to stroke, it would mess up the whole boat, and that's what counts."

So Josh continued to row at seven, fixing his eyes on G.G.'s dark neck instead of on Larry's light one, as the spring days passed and the school year drew to a close.

The Mohican turned from icy to merely chilly. The willows trailed long strands of pale green in the water. All over the school grounds the grass grew thick, strewn with yellow dandelions and with shirt-less boys turning red in the hot sunshine. On the baseball diamonds and tennis courts the players worked up a fine sweat. Even in the cool of the chapel tower the bell ringers perspired as they pulled their ropes in practice for graduation. The bells flung the melody of the school song sweetly over the valley.

> Above the river flowing free
> Stands Oakley School, our Oakley School . . .

Josh heard it on a warm afternoon late in May, walking Indian file across the lower field with Brillo, Scotty Scott, and Ali Mahmud. Scotty was carrying his saxophone and Ali carried the sitar. Josh carried four Cokes and a bag of potato chips. They were heading toward the big oak tree, whose red buds of early spring had now opened into dark green leaves that almost hid the tree house in its branches. It was a special favor to be invited to Brillo's hideaway, and the invitation had inspired a decision to have the long-awaited happening.

The chosen few climbed the struts, Ali coming last with the sitar wrapped in a cloth bag and precariously held at arm's length until Brillo could reach down to haul it to safety. The tree house was complete now, with walls high enough and solid enough to pass Gilly's inspection and with a canvas awning overhead in case of rain.

They settled down cross-legged on the platform, while Ali Baba removed the cloth bag, rested the teakwood gourd against the sole of his foot, and tuned the sitar. "First," he said, "I will play a raga for you. It is music to be played in the spring. We call it *Vasanta*. Then I will show you, any of you, how to play the sitar, if you want." He spoke to all three, but he looked at Josh, because Josh had lost the guitar.

Slipping a metal plectrum on his forefinger, Ali began to play. The delicate notes twanged softly, brightly, and Josh, listening, looked out through the leaves and wished that he could go some day "over the hills and far away" to the strange world that Ali knew well. Oakley School seemed to disappear as the music told of that other world, of its deserts with slowly moving caravans, their camel bells jingling, of jungle flowers and cobras, elephants and monkeys, rajahs, rickshaws and bazaars. Josh had read about such things and now he had a friend, Ali Mahmud, "Ali Baba," whose dark eyes looked homesick for springtime in that faraway land, as his slender fingers plucked the strings of the sitar.

"See," he told them, breaking off in the middle of the raga, "you rest it against your foot like this and hold the strings like this. You want to try?" With a smile, he handed the sitar to Josh. But the sitar was harder than the guitar and would not make the same kinds of tunes. When Josh handed the instrument back, Ali said, "Then I will play and you can all come in with the *tala,* the clap of hands." This arrangement worked very well.

After they had all tried the sitar, Scotty showed what he had learned on the saxophone. He now had perfect command of "Three Blind Mice" and was starting to work on "When the Saints Come Marching In." He had an idea for an Oakley special under the title of "When the Saint Comes Marching In." If he could get someone to sing the words, it ought to be a smash hit with the headmaster next fall, Scotty said. They were trying it when Mr. McGill stepped out of the house and called for quiet. They had waked the baby.

Getting to know Ali was one of the good things that happened to Josh that spring. "You were right about getting to know guys from all over the world at Oakley," he wrote to his mother. "Ali Mahmud

154

has asked me to come to visit him some day. I hope I can. He has taught me to play the sitar a little bit. It is better than the guitar. He speaks four languages. I never believed it, but it is true. I wish I could."

Every day, boys dropped into the room shared by Josh and Larry. They dropped in through the door and they dropped in through the window. With a whole school year behind them, just about everybody in the Fifth Form knew everybody else, and there was a lot to talk about, both the good and the bad experiences that they had shared. Now that they were past, even the bad experiences were something to laugh about together. Next year would be better yet, they determined, and they laid some plans during an important bull session.

Josh said they should be the best class in school next year, the best class Oakley ever had. Dan Garrett said that would be hard, since they would only be the Fourth Form next year, still low and unimportant. Josh said they could have a class project that would make them different. In the high school at home, he said, every class had a project. What kind of a project?

"Oh, clean up the neighborhood, or tutor some little kids, or something like that," Josh told them.

There was silence while everyone present tried without success to think of a neighborhood they could clean up, or some little kids they could tutor at Oakley.

Then Ali Baba said, "There is a school in my village that needs books, pictures, even pencils."

And G.G. Graham said, "There's a Boys' Club in Harlem. When they gave me a scholarship, all their money was used up."

That was the first of several meetings to discuss a class project for next year. The idea caught on in the others classes also and had a side effect in the making of Joshua Cobb. The June issue of the *Oakley Oracle* carried a brief notice of the results of the Fifth Form elections for class officers in the coming autumn: President, Josh Cobb; Vice-President, G.G. Graham; Treasurer, Larry Dunlap; Secretary, Scotty Scott; Class Project Chairman, Ali Mahmud.

Josh wrote to his mother, enclosing the clipping. Then he wrote to Dusty. "I think I made President because I thought up the idea of having a class project and trying to be a really great class instead of just hacking around. G.G. got Vice-President because he is stroke, which is about the best thing you can be at Oakley. He is so good I think he might make junior varsity next year. If he does, I would get a chance to try stroke in *Chingachgook,* that's one of the old shells. My roommate that I told you about is still Treasurer. He really keeps the money straight and not many guys can do that, so we are lucky he wants to. We get along fine now. He helped me in algebra, even more than Mr. McGill. Scotty Scott got Secretary because everybody likes him. Ali Baba should be a good Class Project Chairman. He knows a lot of poor people where he lives in Asia. I think he must be an aristo at home, but here he's just like any other guy.

"Why don't you come sometime? I'd like to show you around. Sincerely, Josh. P.S. If you come at graduation, you'll see me row."

The following week he received Dusty's answer from his Marine base. "Dear Josh, Thanks for the invitation to visit your school. I have a car now and I will be getting two weeks' leave in June. I could come up then, see the school, plus your race, and drive you home. Let me know. Yours in a rush, Dusty."

So it came about that Josh had two special interests among the crowd of visitors arriving at graduation. Helen Crane was coming to see her brother Alan graduate as head prefect of Oakley School. And Dusty Moore would be coming to see the place that Josh had talked about so much at Christmas time. He would drive Josh home. Not everybody was so lucky.

The last days of the school year, like the last days of vacations, went by so fast that Josh remembered them afterward as if they had been a single day, a day of waking in bright sunshine, of attending classes for the last time, of saying goodbye to lots of guys who were now old friends. His Oakley blazer and a new pair of white trousers and white shoes were ready for the graduation ceremony, at which the Fifth Form would lead the whole school into the Yard.

For the First Form, that ceremony was the main event of the day. But for Josh and the other oarsmen the first great event of graduation day was the regatta to be held that morning. When Dusty arrived, doubled up in a small car, Josh could hardly wait for him to extract himself from its interior and unfold his long legs. He still towered above Josh, but not as much as Josh remembered. "You've grown," Dusty said.

"I guess so. Come on," Josh urged. "I'll take you right to Mr. McGill's dock. You're just in time. You can get a good view of the races from there. To see the finish, you'd have to be a mile upstream, but it's O.K. You'll see a lot of the race from the dock."

He reckoned without Brillo, who met them on Gilly's dock and, on being introduced to Dusty, had one of his brilliant ideas. "Why don't we ask Gilly if we can go up to the finish line in the double shell? That is, if you can row?" he inquired.

"Sure thing," Dusty answered promptly. "Been a camp counselor, man and boy, for years." But when, with Gilly's permission, they went to take the double shell from its rack, he looked dubious. "I thought we were going in a boat," he said. "This looks more like a pencil. Oh well, here goes."

Josh left them making their preparations to launch the double shell. He hurried off to join the crew of *Chingachgook* at the boathouse. Scotty was greasing the oars and the crew was standing by to take the shell from the rack. *Uncas* and its crew were afloat, ready and waiting. They looked confident, Josh thought, glancing their way when *Chingachgook* was launched and moving toward midstream.

160

But G.G. was a great stroke. He too was confident, he had good form, he always kept loose, and, best of all, he had the kind of spirit that Swing had talked about, the spark which the whole crew could feel from the leader. Sitting at the number-seven oar behind G.G., Josh felt that will to win. He sensed that the feeling ran from one end of the shell to the other. All was well in *Chingachgook*.

Holding the rudder lines, Scotty leaned forward. "Get ready . . . Ready all . . ." The starting gun. "Row!"

The oar blades dug into the water. Smoothly the two shells began their race, gathering speed with every stroke. No more "like a wounded snake," as Swing had put it, but straight and swift as an Indian arrow sped *Chingachgook*. *Uncas* kept pace, stroke for stroke. Under the bridge and past Gilly's dock they raced, to the sound of cheers all along the shore. If Helen was watching somewhere on the riverbank, if Brillo and Dusty were waiting at the finish line in the double shell, Josh did not know, did not care. One thing mattered, one thing only—to win the race. For this his legs thrust, his arms and back pulled endlessly. "Stroke . . . stroke . . . stroke . . . Take it up to thirty-eight . . . Three-quarter mile . . . stroke . . . stroke . . . 'stroke . . .'"

From the corner of his eye Josh saw *Uncas*. It was falling behind, and this time he knew that *Chingachgook* would not fall apart. Its crew would hold the lead they had won. "Stroke . . . stroke . . . Take it up to forty . . . steady . . ." In response to Scotty's order,

G.G. increased the beat and *Chingachgook* started a final sprint, widening its lead over *Uncas*. But Josh's arms and legs were tiring. He felt his head bobbing backward and forward like a rag doll with every stroke.

Then from behind came Larry's voice, between gasping breaths. "Falling apart . . . Corn Cobb?"

The effect on Josh was instantaneous. He reacted to the mocking words as if the old Josh had jumped into the river and a brand-new one, full of fire, had taken his place. His anger gave him enough energy to pull that oar to the North Pole and back, if need be. Behind the wooden stakes that marked the channel, small boats crowded the river around the finish line as *Chingachgook* sprinted half a length ahead of *Uncas*. In the judges' boat, Swing dropped the flag to signal the end of the race, and Scotty steered his victorious crew a few more yards upstream to let them "wind down."

Larry spoke again. "Sorry about that, but I thought if I made you mad enough, you'd pull yourself together." His voice was friendly—and tired.

Now that he could turn his head, Josh did so. "It worked," he said. "Thanks." And he grinned at his roommate.

From the double shell Brillo and Dusty gave a cheer as the crew of *Chingachgook,* resting on their oars, floated past. In a little clearing on the riverbank a crowd of spectators were gathered to applaud both the victors and the vanquished, and Josh saw Alan

Crane with a girl in a certain yellow sweater that he recognized. They were waving and calling, "Great race!"

Chingachgook and *Uncas* returned to the boat-house, their crews rowing "gently down the stream," relaxing their tired muscles. At the dock, the crew of *Chingachgook* climbed out of their shell, took Scotty by his arms and legs and threw him into the river. After which, with a mighty cheer, they all jumped in. Then both crews cleared the way for the varsity race against a picked crew who might make varsity next year. The varsity won handily, but spectators agreed that the beginners' race between *Uncas* and *Chingachgook* was the exciting one.

On this last day, school already had an unfamiliar look. Nothing was as usual. Boys and parents trekked back and forth, loading cars with suitcases, books, skis, and other unpackables that would not be needed again until fall. In the Yard, the detention squad, as its last duty of the year, was assembling rows of folding chairs on either side of a center aisle, making things ready for graduation. Soon after lunch, parents and friends began to fill the chairs reserved for them at the back.

From the chapel tower a bell chimed the hour. The audience rose, and down the center aisle, in a double column two hundred strong, came the boys of Oakley School. The Fifth Form led the way, filing into the empty seats as they came to them. The Fourth Form followed, then the Third, the Second, and at last the

165

heroes of the day, the First Form, the graduating class, took the seats at the very front.

Now all were standing as the faculty, awesome in black academic robes, moved down the aisle in slow procession, and Josh saw for the first time the splendid silken hoods, draped in bright colors, at the backs of those robes. These men who taught him every day, they knew a lot, more than he would probably ever know. Learning! This, then, was what school was really all about. It was a new idea to Josh, one he must think about when he had time to think.

Meanwhile, the audience sat down, and the student body of Oakley School steamed in their green blazers under the hot sun, while an important man made a speech. Josh did not know who he was and did not take in much of the speech. He was waiting, as were all the rest, for the prizes, and the trophies, and the diplomas. Now, to the sound of polite applause, Mr. St. Clair was shaking the hand of the speaker, and the audience sat up with renewed interest. The real business of the afternoon began. Some of the prizes were scholarships, some were silver cups inscribed with the names of winners and kept at school year after year. Some awards were only words of praise. But all were greeted with cheers and congratulations by the student body and the parents and friends of the winners.

Most of the awards were no surprise to the students. Almost everyone knew who was best in science, in math, in English and French and Latin and history.

They knew the sports heroes. It was no surprise when Alan Crane came forward to receive the Headmaster's Cup for the boy who had made the greatest contribution to Oakley School. But the last award sent a buzz of speculation through the ranks of boys. This was the Faculty Prize, a book, given yearly for what was called Intellectual Curiosity.

"In making this award," said Mr. St. Clair, "the faculty usually chooses someone from the upper forms, but this year for the first time we have chosen a member of the Fifth Form." Electrified, the Fifth Form sat up straighter, tense and expectant. They saw the corners of the Saint's mouth twitch. "The faculty hope," he went on, "that the winner will not take this as a sign of approval for lateness in filling assignments, or for other misdemeanors." Here the twitch broadened into a smile. "But they are unanimous in giving the award, a copy of the *Iliad*, to Igor Brilovich."

It was a great moment for the Fifth Form. A few, like Josh, who were Brillo's special friends, clapped until their hands were sore, glad for his success. Others took notice of him for the first time as someone they would like to know better next year. And those who considered Brillo slightly crazy were pleased to see how many ways there were to win prizes at Oakley School. If there was even a prize for Intellectual Curiosity, whatever that was, surely no one could miss them all!

One by one, each member of the First Form was

167

going up to shake hands with the Saint and to receive his diploma. At this moment it did not seem likely to Josh that he himself would someday be a member of the First Form, receiving a diploma, or possibly even a prize. He could look ahead no further than next fall, when he would be the president of the Fourth Form. That responsibility was plenty. Maybe it was too much—time would tell. But he was willing to try. He had had enough of following. It would be exciting to try leading for once.

From the chapel tower the bells were ringing,

> Yes, we will all be true to thee,
> However long the years may be,
> Still bright and fair in memory,
> Oakley School, our Oakley School.

When it was over and they had all left the Yard, Josh looked for Helen and saw her standing under a tree with Alan Crane. He was saying goodbye to a circle of friends, and Josh skirted around the group until he found an opening to reach her.

"I guess I won't be seeing you for a while," he said, coming straight to the point, "but how about the first dance next year? Will you be my date?"

She looked startled. "That's a long way off," she said.

"I know," he told her, "but I wanted to be sure."

She nodded. "I'll save it."

"Promise?"

"Promise."

A new graduate pushed in front of Josh, shutting him out, but he went off, well-satisfied, to find Dusty.

"I'll get my junk," he said.

On their way to the car, carrying his last load of "junk," they passed Mr. St. Clair. He was mopping his forehead and carrying his academic robe over his arm. Josh stopped.

"This is Dusty Moore," he said, "my counselor from camp. He came to see the school."

"Are you in college?" asked Mr. St. Clair, shaking hands.

"No, still in the service, sir. College next year," Dusty told him.

"Then what?"

"I'd like to teach."

Mr. St. Clair nodded, looking pleased. "When you're ready, come and see me," he said.

With the car loaded, Dusty and Josh squeezed into the few remaining square inches of space, and Dusty started the motor. Slowly they moved away from the deserted school, gathering speed along the road toward town. As they passed Gilly's house, they caught sight of the family. Near the little dock, Mr. and Mrs. Gilly were shellacking the upturned double shell. A baby carriage stood in the shade of the big oak tree. Dusty honked a farewell and Gilly looked up and waved. Suddenly a cream-colored dog tore out of the house and flung himself almost under the wheels of Dusty's car, barking frantically.

"That dumb dog," said Josh. "Keep going. He'll give up."

But they had crossed the bridge over the Mohican and were halfway to town before Winston gave up. When Josh looked back for the last time, the dumb dog was still standing in the road, looking after Josh as long as he could see him.